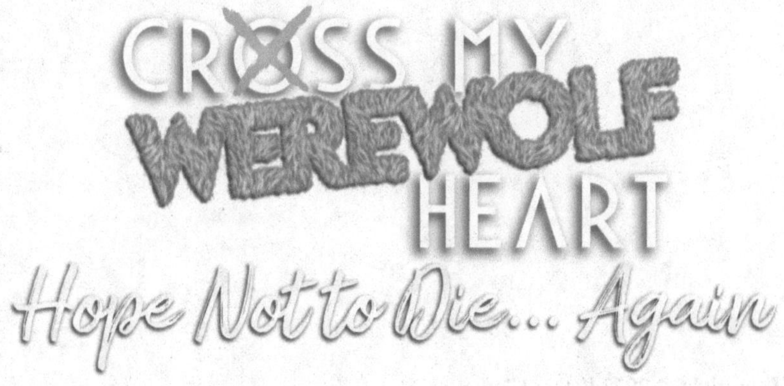

Cross My Werewolf Heart

Hope Not to Die… Again

Series Overview

In the Cross My Werewolf Heart trilogy, Digital Content Manager, Clarissa Hunt's life takes an unexpected turn when she awakens in a body bag after a bizarre accident claims her life. But death is just the beginning of her wild journey.

Tasked with unraveling the mystery of her newfound immortality, Clarissa finds herself thrust into a supernatural world teeming with werewolves, ancient secret societies, and perilous enemies determined to end her life, for good.

As she navigates Melbourne's paranormal underbelly, Clarissa's sense of humor becomes her most valuable asset.

Amidst the chaos, she finds herself caught between a ruggedly handsome yet abrasive stranger, and a charming and alluring doctor, both vying for her romantic attention.

A tale filled with twisty turns, mayhem and mystery, Cross My Werewolf Heart, will have you turning pages faster than xxx, and leave you breathless with anticipation.

•••

Prepare to be enthralled by this fast-paced paranormal romantic comedy set against the backdrop of Melbourne, Australia.

With a comedic flair and a contemporary tone, Cross My Werewolf Heart blends otherworldly shenanigans with laugh-out-loud moments, providing readers with a captivating and entertaining tale.

Join Clarissa on her hilarious and perilous adventure as she confronts monsters, uncovers ancient secrets, and discovers that even in the face of danger, laughter can be the ultimate weapon.

If you love reading Robyn Peterman, MaryJanice Davidson, Cynthia St. Aubin, Carrie Pulkinen and Janet Evanovich, you'll adore sinking your teeth into Esther Del Zuanne's, debut series, Cross My Werewolf Heart.

Cross My Werewolf Heart Hope Not to Die...Again

"For some reason, I thought heaven would look more, I don't know, heavenly."
—Clarissa Hunt, Cross My Werewolf Heart: Hope Not to Die...Again.

•

I was wrong. It could get worse. It could get a whole lot worse... And it did.

Not only has Alpha Werewolf, Silvio De Benedetto disappeared, but now I'm facing the prospect of my first full moon with a werewolf heart.

Would I transform into a snarling, drooling monster and tear up the town—literally? Or would I discover an exciting new paranormal ability to go along with the half dozen or so I'd already developed?

Things get more complicated when I steal my best friend's car following a minor (read: major) personal crisis, and get kidnapped by a coven of disgusting vampires, hell-bent in claiming the hefty blood bounty on my head.

How? How do I keep getting into these ridiculously dangerous situations, when all I want to do is go back to my nice, normal life?

What did I ever do?

Something tells me, though, finally getting to the bottom of the whole saga, and discovering what a werewolf heart truly means for my future, the nice, normal life I long to return to is nothing more than a distant memory.

•

Cross My Werewolf Heart: Hope Not to Die...Again is the thrilling conclusion to the fast-paced, raucously funny and wildly unpredictable Cross My Werewolf Heart trilogy, set in the fantastical world of #fangsfurandfreaks

But don't expect full closure at the end of this book. Nah-uh! There are still plenty of questions surrounding the origin of Clarissa's werewolf heart, and the role it plays in her past, present, and future.

So, keep an eye out for the next exciting instalment in the Werewolf Heart paranormal adventure series, Break My Werewolf Heart, hitting bookshelves and online stores Halloween 2024!

For my sister from another mister, Josephine.

What would I do without you?

*Where would I be without your unwavering support,
encouragement and enthusiasm?*

*How would I have made it through this writing journey, and
come out the other side with not one, not two, but three novels,
without you next to me; cheering me on, standing with me,
shoulder to shoulder, in the thick of it?*

*You are my rock. My voice of reason. My very own pep-squad.
My best friend. My sister. And this one's for you.*

•

*In loving memory of Phillip Camilleri and Vincent Graham.
Always loved. Always remembered. Always in our hearts.*

DISCLAIMER

G'day!

Just a quick note to let you know that, despite being published in USAmerican English, this book contains lots of fun Australian content. It's written by an Australian author, featuring (mostly) Australian characters and is set in Melbourne, Australia.

There are plenty of Aussie turns of phrase, references to Australian celebrities, sporting heroes, retail stores, and places that may be unfamiliar to readers who have never lived in, or visited Australia. These are integral aspects of the story and contribute to its unique charm and fresh flavour (yep, that's flavour with a U #winkwink).

I sincerely hope you enjoy this wild trip Down Under.

ONE

FOR SOME REASON I thought heaven would look more, I don't know, heavenly. Lots of fluffy clouds and chubby cherubs shooting arrows and playing harps. Doves fluttering around doing dovey things. I definitely thought there'd be a big pearly gate with St. Peter ticking off names in his giant book.

Never in a million years did I think heaven would look like my old bedroom.

I had died, right? I hadn't imagined that.

I touched my chest and flinched. There was definitely a wound there, right over my heart; a wound I clearly remembered Sonny inflicting when he skewered me with the silver dagger, twisted it like he was gunning a Harley, and slaughtered me in front of Vincent and a room packed to the rafters with baying, slobbering werewolf and vampire hoards.

Yeah, I'd died.

So, maybe I wasn't in heaven? Maybe I was in hell? No. If I were in hell, there'd be more telemarketers, and *We Built This City* would be playing over the loudspeakers on a twenty-four-hour loop. It wouldn't look like the place a teenager would go to escape from the pressures of daily life—or death.

That's when it dawned on me and I sat bolt upright in bed. MY bed.

It didn't just *look* like my childhood bedroom. It *was* my childhood bedroom, right down to my well-loved edition of *Twilight*. This could only mean one thing. I was in my parents' home and I hadn't forever died at all.

But *hoooooow*?

I clearly remembered Sonny killing me. Proper killing me. Even Azrael had appeared to show me the way to the other side.

Maybe silver wasn't as deadly to werewolves as I'd been led to believe. Silver through the heart = dead lycan, isn't that what Vincent had said? I know I hadn't always gotten my facts straight with all the new paranormal info, but I'm pretty sure that handy tidbit was correct. Isn't that why the dagger had sizzled and burned when it penetrated my heart?

Maybe I had gotten it wrong? Or more likely, someone had been telling me porky pies. It's not like anyone had been completely honest with me of late, so I could have been forgiven for not always being able to separate fact from fiction.

"Good morning, sweetheart," my mother sing-songed, flinging open the bedroom door and scaring the pebbles out of me. "Did you sleep well?"

I stared at her, wide-eyed, mouth gaping, desperately trying to get my bearings. What in the name of Elvis Presley was going on?

Why wasn't I dead?

Why was my mum cheerfully yammering about how I needed to get up before I ran late, and berating me for not having set an alarm?

Why was I at my parents' house?

What was I running late for?

Why wasn't I floating in cotton ball-like splendor, being

serenaded by George Michael and David Bowie—because in *my* heaven, they'd be the entertainment?

Mum pulled open the drapes, and brilliant sunshine streamed through the window and straight into my face, charring my retinas and momentarily dazzling me. "You and Asher must have had a lovely night together. I didn't even hear you come in."

What the hell was she talking about? And what did Ziggy's super-creepy son have to do with anything?

"Would you like me to fix you some breakfast?" she continued, oblivious to my confusion, a broad smile splitting her face. "Or will you just eat in the Qantas Lounge?"

"Um, why would I eat in the Qantas Lounge?" I asked, shading my eyes. I briefly wondered if surgery to reverse welder's flash was a thing, and if it was, could I claim it back on Medicare? Because I was going to be seeing spots for *daaays* after this.

"Surely you're going to have something before your flight. You know you have to eat before you take your Kwells, otherwise..." She screwed up her cute little mama nose.

Of course, I knew I had to eat before I took my Kwells. If I didn't take the Kwells, I got motion sick. Sticky, sweaty, vomitty, pasty, yucky motion sick. It was all kinds of gross. No food, no Kwells. No Kwells, vomitus maximus.

But why did I need the Kwells? And what flight was she talking about?

Maybe I was high? I mean, I could have been drugged. Right?

My mother snapped her fingers in front of my face. "Clarissa, what on earth is the matter with you? You're staring at me like you have no idea what's going on. Are you alright?"

Oh, how did I even begin to answer that?

I tried to refocus and follow what mum was saying. "Sorry. What? Yes, my flight. Right. Because, I'm going somewhere."

Maybe I wasn't high. Maybe I was in pre-heaven. Not purgatory—nothing that dramatic. Maybe I was just in heaven's waiting room, and maybe the flight I was taking would whisk me away to proper heaven?

That sounded much better.

But then, if I was in heaven's waiting room, why was my mother there? Sonny hadn't betrayed her and stabbed her in the heart, too, had he?

Mum planted her hands on her hips and frowned. "What's gotten into you? Your flight leaves in…" She peered at her wristwatch and shook her head. "Four hours, and you're playing silly games."

I forced a laugh, which was about as convincing as my cousin Julie's nose job. (You just knew she and Michael Jackson had the same plastic surgeon.) "You know me." I chuckled. "Always with the silly games."

"Yes, well, you don't have time for games. Move it."

"So, where exactly am I going?" I asked, not entirely sure how I was going to explain why I didn't know my own travel itinerary, but confident I'd be able to come up with something reasonably convincing. I'd become particularly adept at lying on the fly.

"Oh, for heaven's sake. Stop worrying. I've got it all memorized."

Crisis averted.

"Your flight number, your arrival time at Charles de Gaulle, the phone number for the *Grand Hôtel Du Palais Royal*. We're picking Miss Miranda up on the way home, we'll water your plants and collect your mail. Everything is under control, so just go on your holiday, and enjoy."

Holiday? Charles de Gaulle? *Palais Royal*? Was I going to Paris? I loved Paris! Even if it was Paris heaven.

Mum glanced around the room and frowned again. "Where are your bags? Please tell me you've packed."

Did I really need to pack to go to Paris heaven? Aren't togas, or billowy caftans at least, supplied on arrival?

"Just say yes," Poppy whispered in my ear, and I just about peed myself. In fact, it took every ounce of willpower I had not to shriek at the top of my lungs and commando roll out of bed.

"Well?" Mum repeated. "Where are they?"

Poppy nudged me. "Tell her they're in the car and hurry up or you're going to blow this."

I swatted at Poppy, which caught my mother's eye. She peered at me, then shifted her gaze to the left, and if I didn't know better, I could have sworn she looked directly at Poppy. Mum's expression didn't change, nor did her body language, but there was a subtle shift in the way she smelled—like rosemary and muddy puddles. She smelled like damp washing and stale bed linen. Simply, she reeked of sadness. Which would have made perfect sense if she could actually see Poppy. Of course, I knew she couldn't. Azrael had made it crystal clear that humans just don't have that capacity. But could she sense her presence, maybe? Did she instinctively know the spirit of her dead child was hovering less than ten feet away from her? Was it mother's intuition?

Or maybe she just thought I'd developed a weird kind of nervous tic, which she'd Google after I left, and obsess over for the next three months?

"Um, yes, I'm packed," I said, trying to regain her attention. "And my bags are already in the car. I just have to jump in the shower, then I'll be good to go."

Mum looked at me again and touched the base of her throat with her fingertips. "Well thank goodness. For a minute there, I thought you'd—"

That's when my father swanned in, dressed in a royal-blue, velvet tracksuit, Reebok trainers and his favorite Tag Heuer wristwatch. All that was missing were the gold chains and he could seriously have passed as a Goodfella.

"What in the hell is he wearing?" Poppy asked. "It looks like Uncle Julian's old couch cover."

I had to stifle my laugh. Our Uncle Julian was color blind and had all the good taste of a sewer rat. It was hard to believe he was actually Drew's father. Drew had impeccable taste.

"Hey, there's my little lovebird," he said. "Asher tells me the two of you had a fun time. Good for you. What did I tell you? Daddy knows best."

What the hell was he talking about? And why did they keep bringing up Asher?

"They think you went on a date with him last night," Poppy whispered. "Just go with it."

Just go with it? *Go with it?* Was she *crazy*?

"Anyway, sorry I can't drive you to the airport today, princess."

He barely stopped to take a breath.

"But I've got a ten o'clock with the registrar, and I can't wait to see the look on her legal team's face when we throw the book at them. Ziggy has put together quite a brief for your malpractice suit. Could be big money."

"What malpractice suit?"

"They've launched a malpractice suit against the hospital, you know, because of the body bag thing," Poppy said.

"What the hell is going on?" I growled.

Mum blinked at me. "Pardon?"

I shook my head. "It's nothing. Just talking to myself."

"Say," Dad said, completely oblivious to anything else going on around him. "You haven't heard from that doctor from the Myer Clinic, have you?"

"Um, you mean, Dr. Nash?" I replied, my cheeks flushing.

"Or as I like to call him, Dr. Hottie McYummie Pants," Poppy said.

Dad snapped his fingers and pointed at me. "That's him. We've been trying for days but only seem to be able to get through to his answering service. Thought you might know how to get in touch."

"Nope. Haven't talked to him."

Dad frowned.

"Anthony, stop, please," my mother said, resting her delicate hand on my father's velvet-swathed arm. "Can't you see she's still half-asleep? Her flight leaves at midday and she hasn't even eaten yet."

Dad recoiled slightly. "Oh, well, you better do that. You remember the vomiting incident?"

"How could I forget?" I replied and I wondered if I was ever going to live that down. It's not like I'd planned to throw up on the flight attendant. Okay, two flight attendants. And the first aid officer…and several passengers.

"That's settled then. You get dressed and come downstairs when you're ready. I'll poach you an egg."

"It's okay, I'll eat at the—"

"Emily!" my mother bellowed as she left my room and headed toward the kitchen. Emily was her assistant. What a retired primary school teacher needed assistance with, I'll never know, but Mum seemed to keep her busy. "Can you give me a hand with Clarissa's breakfast, please?"

"Qantas Lounge," I said, finishing my sentence, even though Mum had stopped listening.

"Is everything alright?" Dad asked, his brow creasing. "You haven't been yourself since the body bag incident. Not that I blame you. I can't imagine what it was like to wake up in a morgue."

"Technically, I was in the elevator—"

"Don't worry though. Daddy will take care of it all."

I flopped back down on the bed and sighed. "I wish you could. Things have been challenging these past couple of weeks," I confessed. "But it's okay."

I lied.

"Do you need money?" he asked (because Dad's default problem-fixer-upperer was to throw embarrassing amounts of cash at it). "I could transfer—"

I raised my hand. "Thank you but that won't be necessary."

"Are you sure? Forty? Fifty thousand?"

"No, thank you. Really, I'm fine."

"You could treat yourself to a nice facial or maybe a massage? I know a guy." Dad beamed.

"Is the guy Jason Momoa? Because for fifty-thousand dollars, that's who I'd be asking for a massage," Poppy said. "And, if it is him, take Dad up on his offer."

Couldn't argue with that.

My father took two long strides and plonked himself down on my bed, slinging his arm around my shoulders and planting a big, albeit sloppy kiss, on my forehead. "You make sure you let me know if you need anything, princess," he said, ruffling my hair. "There's nothing I wouldn't do for you. You know that, right?"

I nodded. "I know, Daddy."

My father nodded and stood. "Good. You really deserve a break. Go, enjoy your holiday," he said, walking to my bedroom door. "And when you get back, we'll talk, okay?"

"Okay."

He gave me a wave before closing the door behind him.

I swung around and glared at Poppy. "What the hell is going on?" I growled. "And please tell me I didn't really go on a date with Asher!"

TWO

"I CAN'T BELIEVE YOU!" I screamed, jabbing my finger into Sonny's chest in short, sharp stabs. "You're utterly despicable!"

"Stop it!" he said, slapping my hand away. "You're going to leave a bruise."

"I'm going to do more than leave a bruise, you...you...you…" I couldn't think of a word horrible enough to describe exactly just how vile Sonny was.

Mum and her driver, Armando—an 80-something Uruguayan man who'd worked for my parents longer than I'd been alive—dropped me off at Tullamarine Airport at a little after 10 a.m. Part of me was hoping I really was jetting off to Paris, but alas, it was just another ruse cleverly orchestrated by Vincent, and his band of merry assholes. Instead of boarding a flight to Charles De Gaul, I was bundled into a POO Uber—or would it be called a POOber?—and whisked back to the cathedral.

Just another big, fat lie perpetrated by the Kings of Big Fat Lies.

Poppy had traveled with me in the back of the town car and blabbered on for the entire trip. Mum had remained uncharacteristically quiet, and if I hadn't known better, I could have sworn she was listening to her first-born child explain how I'd come to be back at home, tucked up in my bed, after being killed by Sonny.

Apparently, the POOs had enlisted the services of a *kadji*, an Aboriginal shaman or *clever man* to fabricate memories and implant them into my parents' subconscious to explain away my presence at home. Apparently, the new memories involved me going on a date with Asher, which meant he and Ziggy had been party to the mind-wipe exercise, too. FML. This *kadji* was the same person they'd used to *take care of* my poor, unsuspecting neighbors following the Beverley incident.

I hope they had the *kadji* on retainer.

The more I learned about the POOs, the less I wanted to know, but I also understood them more than I cared to admit, because the parallels between the Patrons and my dad were... well, let's just say there were a lot. Their approaches might have differed, but the motivations were the same. The POOs threw their weight around by means of magic and deception, and mind-altering *kadji*. My father threw his weight around by means of large deposits of cash, convoluted legal cases, and a sleaze ball lawyer who only had dollar signs in his eyes, and a son whom I was now dating, apparently. Double FML.

They were more alike than even I cared to acknowledge. I couldn't even begin to imagine the horrors if the POOs and my dad ever decided to collab.

I'd been seated in Vincent's office for what felt like forever, stewing in my own rage, and wondering why they'd brought me back.

I'd expected there'd be groveling and apologies and explanations and possibly gifts.

I liked gifts. Jewels, designer handbags, ice cream.

What I hadn't expected, however, was for Sonny to come flouncing in, all handsome and sexy and charming…the murderous, duplicitous, Judas, turncoat, Benedict Arnold, Brutus he was. Of course, the first thing I did when I clapped eyes on him was surge to my feet and lunge across the room.

"You stabbed me," I screeched.

"I know. No need to thank me."

My mouth dropped open. "You're kidding, right? You stabbed me IN THE HEART WITH A SILVER DAGGER! Why on earth would I thank you, you asshat?"

"You need to settle down and listen," he said.

"I don't have to do anything you say," I screamed, then choked back the tears I refused to shed in his presence. "You of all people were never meant to hurt me. You were meant to protect me from all those weirdos. I knew *they* wanted to kill me, even a doorknob could read that room, but I would never have imagined, not in a million years that *you* wanted to kill me."

"I didn't *want* to kill you. I *had* to."

"Had, schmad. I call bullshit."

My mind was awash with confusion and anger and wow, pain I'd never experienced. Yet all the while, Sonny's face remained impassive, focused.

The large oak office doors swung open, and Vincent strode in, long cashmere coat billowing behind him as he stormed toward us. Judging by the look on his face, he was not amused.

"Am I interrupting something?" he asked, coming to a stop directly in front of us, his brow creased.

We must have looked quite the sight, me with my crazy, blotchy face (I tend to get sweaty and horrible when I'm over-stimulated) and, oh God, my hair. I'd have wagered $1,000 that I looked like Robert Smith from The Cure. Then there was Sonny, pouting like a scolded three-year-old, gingerly rubbing the spot on his chest I'd been poking.

"No, actually you're just in time to watch me beat the stuffing out of Sonny," I growled.

Sonny threw his hands in the air. "I think someone is overreacting just a smidge, don't you?"

I swung back to face him. "I'll give YOU overreacting." My hand shot out, lightning fast, catching Sonny by the throat and shoving him so hard against the wall that tiny puffs of plaster dust whirled around us like microscopic snowflakes. The walls seemed to groan and bow in response to the impact.

"Clarissa! Stop this at once!" Vincent yelled. "You're hurting him, not to mention destroying my office."

"But I *want* to hurt him," I replied, squeezing ever so slightly, disappointed when there was no gurgling or gasping for air on Sonny's part. He didn't even make a grab for my hands or attempt to convince me to release my grip. It would have been pointless anyway, because I wasn't about to let go. Maybe if I squeezed a little harder…

"I insist you release him this minute and explain to me what on earth is going on," Vincent demanded.

"No," I replied.

I felt the familiar weight of Vincent's hand on my shoulder. He leaned in close and lowered his voice, whispering in my ear, "Let him go before I make you let him go. I won't tell you again."

I turned toward Vincent, ready for a full-on staring competition which, FYI, I was practically a world champion at because Miss Miranda and I had them often—generally due to some kind of food-related stand-off—and I *always* won.

Well, maybe not *always*, but most of the time.

Okay, sometimes.

Fine, never, but in my defense, she was particularly good at not blinking when she was peeved and hungry.

What struck me immediately, though, was the color of Vincent's eyes. They had transformed from their usual charcoal to a blazing amber that, while quite stunning, was also deeply disturbing.

"Clarissa, I'm serious." There was a quiet authority in Vincent's tone that sent a chill down my spine. Yes, it was terrifying, but was it terrifying enough for me to let go of the bastard who'd killed me?

As I saw it, I had two options:

1. I could continue to squeeze Sonny's neck until it either snapped or I crushed his windpipe, and risk Vincent decapitating me and setting my headless corpse on fire.

Can't say I liked that option.

1. Or I could let go, eliminate the need for Vincent to inflict grievous bodily harm for now, and then finish killing Sonny later.

I opted for the latter, giving one last squeeze before releasing Sonny. Five perfect fingernail marks punctured his neck, and I felt a strange sense of satisfaction at the sight of my handiwork.

"She's crazy," Sonny croaked, rubbing his neck.

I scowled at him.

"Would either of you care to tell me what's going on?" Vincent asked, crossing his arms over his chest. "I could hear the ruckus all the way up in my chambers."

"Sure. I can explain. Butt-face here killed me," I snarled, jutting my chin at Sonny.

"Butt-face? Seriously, what are you, twelve?" Sonny snorted.

"What if I am? I was still kicking your ass," I replied, trying to ignore the effect Sonny's close proximity was having on my body. My brain might have been screeching to gut him like a fish, my body, however, thrummed to life in his presence. Stupid, treacherous body.

"Try it again. I dare you." Sonny squared his shoulders and puffed out his impressive chest like the bulging Neanderthal he was.

"Clarissa, if Sonny wanted to kill you, I can assure you, he would have by now," Vincent said.

"But he *did* kill me," I snapped.

"I meant *really* kill you. Forever kill you."

Sonny smiled smugly. "You should listen to the man, Clarissa. He's right."

I bristled.

Vincent sighed and stepped between us, placing a hand firmly on each of our chests. "I strongly suggest the two of you just settle down and explain what's going on."

I stepped away and crossed my arms, adding an extra foot or so between me and Sonny. He was so lucky Vincent was there, or there was a good chance they'd need to bring in the super-max cleaning crew just to scoop up all the itty-bitty pieces of Sonny that remained after I tore him up.

"What's this all about?" Vincent's eyes had returned to their usual onyx, which I have to say, was quite the relief. I made a mental note to ask him about the whole changing eye color thing some other time when I wasn't plotting Sonny's demise.

"Are you kidding me? You were there. You saw it with your own eyes. He killed me," I said, pointing at Sonny. "He plunged a silver dagger into my heart and killed me."

"Yes, I'm aware of that."

"In my defense, it was a silver-plated letter opener, not a dag—"

Vincent and I both turned and glared at Sonny.

"You're not helping," Vincent chastised.

I stared at Vincent and waited for the fury to set in. Any minute, he would explode into a tirade that would leave Sonny quaking in his Doc Martens. *What possessed you to do this to her?* he'd admonish. *Your behavior was completely unacceptable and reprehensible. Pack your bags, bud. You're outta here!* A dozen potential scenarios raced through my mind, each more satisfying than the previous.

So, I waited.

And waited.

And waited for Vincent to explode.

But he didn't.

Nothing.

Not so much as a peep.

"You did hear what I said, right?" I asked, snapping my fingers near Vincent's ear. "You haven't gone deaf all of a sudden?"

"No, I haven't." He swatted my hand away. "I assure you I heard every word."

"So why aren't you flipping your shit? Why aren't you giving Mr. Stabby here a dressing down and threatening to lock him up in the Dungeon of No Wi-Fi?" I barked.

Vincent eyed Sonny, his mouth thinning. "Sonny, do you have something you need to tell me?"

Sonny dropped his gaze. "Nope."

"Why do I get the feeling that's not entirely true?" Vincent asked.

"Because it isn't. He's full of shit," I replied, sneering at Sonny.

"Clarissa, if you don't mind, I'll take care of this."

I scowled but decided to shut my mouth and see how things panned out.

"Sonny, did you or did you not inform Ms. Hunt of the plan to assassinate her at the gathering of the Patrons?"

Sonny didn't reply. He just kept studying his shoes.

"Um, plan?" I asked.

"I'm waiting," Vincent said, ignoring me.

"No, I did not," Sonny said.

"I'm sorry, but did you say, *plan*?" There was that shrill tone again. "*What plan?*"

"There was a plan, a plan devised purely with your safety in mind," Vincent said.

"A plan to kill me?"

Vincent nodded.

"And you *knew* about this?" I glared at Vincent. "You *let* it happen?"

Sonny did this weird cough-laugh thing, and Vincent shot him a greasy look.

"Well, yes," Vincent said, calmly. "I was aware that Sonny intended to kill you at the gathering of the Patrons."

"*Aaaand...*" Sonny said. "Tell her the rest."

Vincent cleared his throat and glared at Sonny.

"Hey, if I'm going down, I'm taking you with me," Sonny said.

"Go on. You might as well get it all out in the open." I was suddenly overwhelmed by a wave of emotional exhaustion. I was just so tired of all the secrets and the scheming and the *craaaaap* these people kept putting me through. I must have been a world-class masochist to keep coming back for more. "I want to know just how big a bunch of assholes you actually are."

I'd never seen Vincent uncomfortable before. He got this strange little crease between his eyebrows and the corner of his mouth twitched ever so slightly.

"Well," he said. "The reason I'm not flipping my shit, as you so eloquently put it, is because I may have been the one to suggest that maybe, it might be a good idea for Sonny to kill you."

It took a few seconds for my brain to register what Vincent had said. He'd ordered Sonny to kill me. *He* had.

"You, *what*?" I screeched, finding my voice again.

"He ordered me to kill you," Sonny repeated, slowly and deliberately. "Who's the deaf one now?"

"Why would you do that? *Why*?"

"An order is an order," Sonny said. He didn't even have the decency to look at me.

"Was I talking to you?" I snapped.

"Clarissa, please calm down and allow me to explain." Vincent's voice was low and soothing, exactly what I needed to tip me right over the edge and into the abyss of insanity.

"*Calm down*? If that's not the dumbest thing you could have said to me right now. When in the history of *EVER* has telling someone to calm down resulted in someone actually calming down?"

Sonny shrugged. "She has a point."

"Again," I said, turning on Sonny. "Not. Talking. To. You."

Sonny raised his hands and took a step backward.

"Faking your death was a plan I devised to get the Patrons off our backs long enough to work out what to do about you," Vincent said.

"It seemed like a really good idea at the time," Sonny added.

"Seemed like a good idea at the time? What to *do* about me? Do you even hear yourselves? Are you *insane*?" I shrieked. "Of course, you're insane. You're both off your goddamn rockers. You know you're lucky I don't ring both your scrawny little necks—"

"Baby, there's nothing scrawny about any part of me," Sonny said.

I launched myself at Sonny, reaching for his shirt collar, but Vincent stuck out his arm, quicker than the eye could see, and caught me mid-lunge.

"Don't you touch me," I said, pushing Vincent away. "You're both horrible."

"Enough!" Vincent barked. "One more outburst and I promise *neither* of you will live to regret it. Am I clear?"

I stood back and nodded, still eye-balling Sonny.

"I can't hear you."

"Crystal," I said.

"Thank you," Vincent added before turning his attention to Sonny. "Now, please explain to Clarissa why it was in her best interest for the Patrons to believe she was dead, for the time being, at least." Vincent turned and faced me again and waved his index finger around in front of my face. "And you had better keep your mouth shut while Sonny explains, or I promise, I will kill you myself."

"And he'll do the forever kind of killing, too," Sonny added. "Not the half-assed attempts you've experienced so far."

"They've all felt pretty real to me," I said, raising my fingers to my chest, still smarting from when Sonny had stabbed me.

"Firstly, let me just clarify your life was never in any danger," Sonny said. "We all know that, so let's get a little perspective."

"Says the man who stabbed me in the heart," I mumbled. "Perspective, my ass."

Sonny sighed. "The truth is, we really don't know much about your situation. Clarissa," he said. "We need more time. Time to work out how this all happened; why the transplant operation was successful on you when it failed on so many others. We need to understand what long-term effects an active werewolf heart could have on a human. We need time to learn which werewolf traits you'll develop, and what effects they might have on you mentally and physically. So, we did what we had to do to get the Patrons off our backs."

"By stabbing me? Good plan," I said, giving him the double thumbs-up. "What if I'd actually died? I mean, like *forever* died."

"But you didn't, did you? In fact," Sonny said, pushing himself off the wall he'd been leaning against and taking a couple of long, slow strides in my direction. "You've barely got a scratch on you. You're practically all healed, healthy as an ox, and best of all, the werewolves and vampires now think you're out of the picture."

"Now, isn't that impressive?" Vincent beamed.

"I think the word you're looking for is *barbaric*," I corrected.

"Yes, yes, of course. Barbaric, most certainly." For someone whose life depended on lying, Vincent really wasn't all that convincing. "Still, don't you think it was a teensy-weensy bit clever…in a way?"

I chose to ignore him.

"And now," Sonny continued as if I weren't even there. "We are in a position to get to the bottom of your situation."

Even though I knew he wouldn't, part of me was still waiting for Vincent to recoil in horror, but there was no recoiling. In fact, I'd say he was looking quite pleased with himself.

"Sonny was instructed to advise you of the plan, however, but it seems he neglected to complete that part of his assignment," Vincent said. "Something I'm still waiting on an explanation for."

"Oh, come on, I couldn't tell her, and you know it." Sonny pointed at Vincent. "As much as we would have liked to believe we had everything under control, we didn't. The Patrons would have smelled a rat a mile away. For the plan to succeed, we needed her to not know, to make it look more authentic. So, in my position as Chief Peacekeeper, I withheld the information."

I scowled at both of them. "You know what? I hate you both. I died and you two schmucks are slapping each other on the back like you're the fucking Justice League? Well guess what? You," I pointed at Sonny, "are no Superman. And you." I pointed at Vincent. "You are no Iron Man."

"Actually," Sonny said. "Iron Man is Marvel not DC, so a more accurate comparison would be—"

"*Seriously?*" I said, Vincent and I both rolled our eyes.

"I don't know who I'm angrier at, you for killing me." I pointed at Sonny. "Or you for coming up with the cockamamie idea in the first place." I pointed at Vincent.

"But it was a good idea, Clarissa. Simple, effective," Sonny replied.

"No, numb-nuts, it wasn't a good idea. It was reckless and cruel and shows neither of you has any respect for me, my well-being or any regard whatsoever for my feelings." To my horror, big, fat tears rolled down my cheeks and dripped off my chin. "I could have *DIED*, and neither of you seem to understand that or even care."

"I never would have let you die, Clarissa." Sonny extended his hand and stepped forward. His expression softened and his voice took on an almost caring tone. Clearly, I was having an auditory hallucination, because the day Sonny was nice to me would be the day I went on a date with Asher—for real. "I stepped in, and while killing you was an unorthodox approach, I actually saved your life because you were in grave danger."

There it was again; that caring tone. What was with that?

"Those bloodsuckers and lycanthropes were getting ready to finish you off, right there and then. I couldn't let that happen. Wouldn't. You're too important." Wait, was he *blushing*? "To the Patrons, of course."

"Of course." I nodded, my bullshit meter totally redlining. "To the Patrons."

"And if I had to, I'd do it all again."

THREE

"WHAT'S GOING ON?" I asked, trying to maneuver around Sonny and get a better view of the scene unfolding in the grand foyer.

I chose to visit POO central, even though Vincent and Sonny had banished me to my room. Okay, that might be an exaggeration, but they had told me to stay home and keep a very low profile.

I think we all know that was never going to happen.

Sneaking into the cathedral wasn't exactly keeping a low profile, but it's not like I was doing Facebook lives from Federation Square now was it? And besides, if I'd stayed home, I never would have stumbled onto whatever ultra-important POO powwow that was going on.

From my covert vantage point, I caught a glimpse of a stunning woman wearing a gorgeous Cocoon Wrap Coat in seafoam that I'm pretty sure was from the last Victoria Beckham collection. She was standing with Vincent, and I immediately recognized her as Donatella De Benedetto. She was once again flanked by four ridiculously large gargoyle goons, a couple of whom I recognized from the infamous stabby-stabby meeting of the POOs.

Sonny glanced at me, then back at Donatella and Vincent, did a double take, and blanched.

"*Shhhhhit*," he hissed, pulling me aside and shoving me behind a massive concrete planter that was home to a rather impressive Ficus. It was huge, twice as tall as Sonny minimum, and I briefly wondered if it might be the beanstalk from *Jack and the Beanstalk*, because let's face it, anything was bloody possible in that place.

"When did you get here?" Sonny whispered.

"Just now," I said, a little offended he hadn't at least sensed me, or smelled me—no, not smelled me. That would have been gross. I mean, shouldn't he have felt a disruption in the Force or something? Especially considering how acutely aware I was of him, his movements, his scent (the good type of yummy pheromone scent, not the icky stale BO type of scent).

I really had to get over myself, didn't I? While I could now admit I was into him, the same couldn't be said the other way around. I was a job to him, nothing more, and nothing less. But for me, he was becoming so much more.

"What are you even 'oh shitting' about, anyway?" I asked, standing on my tippy toes again. I barely managed to catch a glimpse of Donatella as she greeted Vincent with a polite kiss on each cheek. My God, she absolutely dripped with old Hollywood style and glamour, with her designer clothes, flawless skin, and raven hair wrapped effortlessly into a loose chignon.

No wonder Sonny couldn't take his damn eyes off her. She was just his type, or what I'd imagined his type to be. She was every guy's type—curvy, classy, and sexy. That's when it dawned on me and I shrunk back into the shadows.

"You had a thing with her, didn't you?" I huffed.

"Who?" Sonny asked, still ogling Donatella and every little move she made. *Discretion, Sonny. Discretion.*

"What do you mean, who? Gargoyle number two, who do you think?"

"What?"

"Donatella?" I whispered, pointing in her general direction, suddenly feeling every bit like a Birkenstock accidentally placed on display at Louboutin on Collins. "You dated her."

"I wouldn't exactly call it dating," he replied.

"Oh, that's so much better," I said, my mind instantly conjuring a whole suite of sordid images featuring Sonny and Donatella in the throes of passion.

Stupid, overactive imagination.

"You need to get out of here. Now," Sonny said.

"Tell me about it," I replied.

"No, I'm serious. You have to go."

"Cramping your style, am I?"

"*What?*"

"Never mind," I grumbled. "I know when I'm not wanted."

"What's wrong with you?" Sonny snapped. "Why are you even here? I thought I gave you very explicit instructions—"

"Instructions? What am I, a German Shepherd?"

"Don't start." He crossed his arms over his chest. "Why are you here?"

"I got bored at home," I said.

He raised his brows.

"Lonely."

"Why are you here, Clarissa?"

"Fine. Poppy was driving me nuts, and I needed a latte."

Sonny took a deep breath. "I'm sorry being stuck in a three-story town house with unlimited Wi-Fi and endless snacks is such a strain on you."

"Could you be a little more condescending?" I asked.

"Probably."

"Douche."

Sonny scowled. "You can't just go wandering around wherever you want, Clarissa. We can't let any of these people see you," he growled. "They think you're dead, and it needs to stay that way."

"Maybe I'm my ghost?" I said with a grin.

Sonny rolled his eyes. "You do realize if anyone sees you, the dagger, stabbing you, Azrael and his whole 'it's time to go, Clarissa' routine, will all have been for nothing."

"How was I supposed to know she'd be here?" I said, pointing at Donatella. "I didn't mean—*wait, Azrael*? Azrael was in on it, too?" My voice went up several octaves. Again.

"Of course. Surely he told you—oh." Sonny snapped his mouth shut. "No. Azrael had no idea. He had nothing to do—"

"I swear I'm going to kill him," I seethed.

"See, this is why you were meant to stay home and keep a low profile."

"So you wouldn't accidentally give away any more sordid secrets about just how crappy my friends are?"

"For one."

"Great, I get punished because you can't keep your trap shut. Magical."

"Punished? Who's punishing you? We were protecting you—"

"Sonny!" Vincent barked so loud, his voice echoed like a gunshot through the foyer. "Come here!"

Sonny spun around like a top, but not before he tucked me farther behind the planter. "In a minute," he said.

"Now! I need you to join me and Signorina De Benedetto in my office," Vincent ordered. "It seems we have a problem."

"You think you've got a problem? I'm the one with the damn problem," I grumbled. "I got a massive knife sticking out of my back—a figurative knife, this time—courtesy of my so-called friends. How's that for a problem?"

"Just shoosh," Sonny said, swatting at me.

"Why don't you shoosh?"

"Shut up," Sonny said through gritted teeth. "And don't move."

"Did you hear me?" Vincent yelled, louder this time.

Sonny nodded. "Yes. I did. I just…I just need a minute—"

Vincent excused himself and stalked over to where we were standing. Okay, so Sonny was standing, I was cowering behind a giant Ficus like a gutless wonder.

"Stop playing games, Sonny," Vincent growled. "Go to my damned office and wait for me there."

"Yes, Vincent. Coming right now."

"And you," Vincent said, reaching around and yanking me out from behind the planter. He was surprisingly spry for someone who'd celebrated a millennium…*twice*. "Get the hell out of here before someone sees you and I'll be forced to kill you —permanently."

"Okay, I get it," I said. "I'm sorry."

"Don't apologize," Vincent scolded. "Just do as you're told. Oh, and never disobey a direct order again. Understood?" He didn't actually give me a chance to answer, just turned on his heel and strode back to Donatella. "Coming, Sonny?"

Sonny tutted at me. "Please go home and wait for me. I'll come see you after I've finished up here, okay?"

I nodded and stared at my shoes. "I really am sorry."

Interesting factoid: I actually *was* sorry.

Sonny placed his hands on my shoulders and gently squeezed. "Don't be sorry, Clarissa. Just be careful," he said before planting a kiss on my forehead, turning and following Vincent into his office.

Oh, what that man did to me.

•

I didn't go straight home after leaving POO HQ.

As if.

Instead, I swung past Drew's to see if he fancied a quick brunch at The Pantry before I skulked back to my office to concentrate on work for the rest of the afternoon.

Drew was happy to accommodate, thankfully, so I got to enjoy my first smashed avo on sourdough in what felt like forever. A little cracked pepper, some sea salt, a shot of espresso with two sugars. Bliss.

Afterward, I phoned my parents (who still thought I was in Paris). Dad was headed out to Kingston Heath to play nine holes with Ziggy, and my mum was off to her monthly Zonta meeting, which left me to face the harsh reality of my dismal work situation.

I'd been doing a spectacular job of neglecting my business for weeks, and if I didn't pull my finger out and get my clients' engagement up by 4-5 percent, pronto, I'd lose all of them, along with my town house, and what little was left of my dignity. I'd probably end up back at my parents' place, living in my old bedroom and not qualifying for unemployment benefits.

Of course, instead of working—screw my clients, my business, and my dignity—I sat in my living room, listening to Poppy drone on about *MAFS*, while I stewed in my own juices. Hours had passed since I'd left Sonny at POO headquarters. He'd promised to let me know what was going on with Donatella and the super-important meeting with Vincent, but the day had dragged on and not so much as a peep from Sonny.

I'd worked myself up into quite a state while I was waiting.

I was miffed.

Well, I wasn't so much miffed as I was in a teeny tizz, a quasi-tizz.

A total tizz.

Fine, I was in a frenzy, and what really annoyed me was that I knew my mood had less to do with finding out why

Donatella had paid Vincent an impromptu visit at the cathedral, and more do to with wondering what she was doing at that moment…and whether that something may or may not have involved whipped cream, fluffy handcuffs, and a certain Peacekeeper.

It was a little after midnight when Sonny finally knocked on my door. Of course, the first thing I did before I even opened it was usher Poppy up to her room. Yes, she had a room now. A room with an en suite and walk-in wardrobe, a smart sixty-seven-inch flat screen mounted on the wall opposite her king bed, and full access to all my streaming services. Her undead existence was not too shabby.

As always, she complained as she floated up the stairs to what used to be my home office, grumbling about something. Being treated like a kid, maybe? But that's why I gave her her own private space, so at least she didn't have to spend all her time floating endlessly in the ether. It was all about privacy and comfort and absolutely nothing to do with guilt in any way, shape, or form.

That was my story. I was sticking to it.

Seeing Sonny's massive frame fill my doorway was breathtaking to say the least. Come to think of it, all of him was pretty breathtaking; from the shaggy mop of sandy hair on his beautiful head, all the way down to the heels of his black biker boots. He was just one giant ball of yippee! Not that I was about to let him know that.

"What took you so long?" I asked.

He looked me up and down and smiled appreciatively. "I remember that outfit. You were wearing it the night we met."

I looked down at my trusty old Guns 'N' Roses t-shirt and favorite track pants, that had somehow survived the werewolf fracas in my dining room (or maybe the clean-up crew fixed it?) and was immediately transported back to our first meeting. The shock of finding a stranger in my kitchen, the heat in his eyes when he saw me in my sleep-shirt, the tingly feeling I got when our eyes met. The werewolf. The dying.

Okay, so not all of it was pleasant.

"I was wearing part of it," I said.

"I still like it."

I felt my cheeks flush. "Thanks."

I let Sonny in and showed him to the living room. "Drink?" I asked, walking over to the liquor cabinet, opening a bottle of Glenlivet, and pouring myself a substantial shot.

"Definitely," he said. "Make it a double?"

"Sure." I grabbed a second glass. "Ice?"

He shook his head, flopping down on the couch, and giving Miss Miranda a scratch on the head when she presented herself for pats. What was it with that damn cat? She loved everyone but me these days.

I joined Sonny on the couch and handed him the whiskey, which he downed before I'd even had the chance to taste mine.

He stood. "Mind if I have another?"

I gestured to the liquor cabinet. "Help yourself."

I couldn't remember seeing Sonny so preoccupied. He was generally pretty calm. Well, not calm necessarily; calm*ish*. Almost rational. Even when he was killing me or spinning some fanciful tale, he was usually cool and quick with a smarmy comment or playful remark. I'd seen him angry, bemused, flustered, and frustrated, but I'd never seen him stressed. It was freaking me out a little.

When he eventually made his way back to the couch, he threw his head back against the headrest and closed his eyes.

"Tough day at the office, dear?" I said, still nursing my first whiskey. I'd suddenly lost the taste for it. "Care to share?"

Sonny stretched his arm across the back of the couch, and I sat forward with a jolt.

He opened his eyes and faced me. "Problem?"

I felt my cheeks heat. "No."

"Then why so jumpy?"

"I'm not… I wasn't… I…"

"Did you think I was making a move on you?" His grin was wide and dazzling.

"Ha ha. Nooooo." Could I have sounded any lamer? "I did not."

"Would you *like* me to make a move on you?"

"What? No. Of course not. Yuck."

"Yuck?" he echoed. "Really?"

"Yes. No. I just… I thought… You know what? Just—" I exhaled. "Forget it. Just tell me what you came here to tell me, or I'll just start constructing my own scenarios."

Which I already had.

Sonny peered at me for a second, and I could practically see the cogs in his brain turning. I desperately wanted to know what he was thinking but still had no idea how to get a read on him. Eventually, he took another sip of whiskey and rested his head back on the headrest. "Silvio is missing."

"Silvio De Benedetto?" I said, sitting up and regaining my taste for the whiskey. "What happened?"

"No one knows for sure. He had a meeting scheduled with some real estate developer three days ago, but he never made it. Nobody's seen or heard a peep from him since."

My stomach sank. "Kidnapped?"

Sonny shrugged. "Possibly. Or murdered. We have no idea yet." He exhaled.

"First Dante and now Silvio. Someone really doesn't like that family," I said.

"Donatella is beside herself."

Hmph. I bet she was. I bet she was so upset, the only place she could find comfort was in Sonny's delightfully muscled arms, the floozy.

I was not jealous.

I was not insecure.

I was not paranoid.

I was just a girl, sitting on a couch, drinking eighteen-year-old whiskey, talking shop with a colleague. A hot colleague, with a propensity for shady dealings and killing me.

I needed to get a grip.

"Who do you think is responsible?" I asked, clearing my throat. "Is it Donatella? I bet it's Donatella."

So much for not being jealous.

"What? No. Why would you even suggest her?"

"Because she's prickly, and probably quite ambitious. Plus, she made it crystal clear she doesn't like me, which is mental because *everyone* likes me."

Sonny's brows shot up.

"Fine. Most people like me."

His brows stayed up.

"Fine. I don't like her."

"And none of that has anything to do with you thinking she and I had a thing?"

"Didn't you?"

"I don't kiss and tell."

"Right."

"I could always kiss you and you could find out for yourself, if you like?"

"Pfft. I don't think so. I'd rather kiss a troll."

I. WAS. SUCH. A. LIAR.

"I can arrange that." He smiled.

I sculled my whiskey and coughed as the single-malt liquor hit the back of my throat. "That won't be necessary."

"Suit yourself." He shrugged.

I fanned myself. For a smooth drop, that whiskey practically melted my esophagus. I was going to sound like Marlon Brando for a week.

"You were saying?" I wheezed.

Sonny rubbed his eyes with his thumb and forefinger. "We

think vampires are responsible for taking both Silvio and Dante. They stand to gain the most."

"How so?"

"It's genius, really," he said. "Make the current lycan hierarchy unstable and facilitate a coup to bring down the De Benedetto legacy. Then, install a regime that's more sympathetic to the old ways, chaos ensues, and the world as we know it —*poof*!" He snapped his fingers. "Gone."

"Erm, okay." I didn't understand any of what he said. "And why would they do that?"

He looked at me with a soft expression that looked like he was being condescending but didn't exactly feel that way. "Things haven't always been the way they are now, Clarissa. There was a time, a much darker time, when the Inner World ruled all the realms." He paused and took another swig of his drink.

"Let me guess, it wasn't all wine and puppies?"

Sonny shook his head. "It was utter mayhem—rivers of blood, torture, carnage, destruction. The humans were treated like animals. I mean the ones who weren't hunted down and slaughtered for sport, that is."

"Sounds delightful."

"Couldn't be further from the truth."

"But *why*?"

"There are some species, more aggressive, power-hungry ones that tend toward anarchy and would welcome a return to those dark times."

"Let me guess, the werewolves and vampires?"

"To name a few."

"And what does this have to do with Silvio or Dante?"

"As alpha, Silvio has been instrumental in negotiating a treaty between the Inner and Outer Worlds. Through the Patrons, he and Dante lead the change, whereby all creatures were valued equally, where everyone had the right to a safe and peaceful existence."

"He believed if we all shared, the world would be a better place?" I asked.

Sonny looked at me and smiled. Have I ever mentioned his dimples? His sexy, super-cute dimples?

"You really can distill complex issues, can't you?" he asked.

I shrugged. "I call 'em as I see 'em."

"You sure do."

"There's something I don't understand, though," I said.

"And what's that?"

"Silvio is a lycan, and not just any lycan, he's like the king of the lycans, yet he respects human life."

"And you're wondering why?"

I nodded.

Sonny paused, as if he was trying to frame his response carefully. "Silvio has led a long and interesting life. He's spent a lot of time with humans, grown fond of them, even. There's even a rumor of a romantic entanglement or two, before he married, of course."

"Really?"

"Yep, and as a result, he and his family value life, all life, equally. Other lycans do not."

"Paranormals are awful creatures, aren't they?"

"Not all. Some of us think humans are pretty great." He winked at me and I felt my face heat, again. Geez, who was I? Rebecca? Was I suddenly developing that weird blushing/sweating thing she did whenever Sonny's around?

Thankfully, if he noticed, he didn't say anything.

"Gnomes, sprites, Fae, nymphs, they generally have no desire to end human existence."

"Wait, aren't Fae the super-scary, mega-warrior types?"

He raised a brow. "Who told you that?"

"You did," I replied. "And Vincent."

"Well, that's true, but Fae prefer a peaceful coexistence to war."

"And what about your species? Where do you land, peaceful coexistence or kill, crush, destroy?"

I peered at him hopefully.

"Your detective skills suck, anyone ever tell you that?" he jibed.

"Anyone ever told you all the secrecy around your cultural heritage is stupid?"

"Stupid?"

"Yes, stupid."

"Stupid is as stupid does."

"What does that even mean, Forrest?"

"No idea." He shrugged. "But if it's good enough for Mr. Gump—"

I groaned. "Enough, please. I just can't tonight. I'm exhausted."

Sonny ruffled my hair, then rested his hand on my shoulder. Slick. "I know it seems counterintuitive," he said. "But most paranormal species are peaceful. They prefer to live together in harmony."

"Orrrr…"

"Or what?"

"They're waiting for their moment in the sun, or in the darkness, or whatever, lulling humans into a false sense of security, before ripping out our throats while they sleep."

He snorted. "Okay, well, I guess that's also possible."

"Again, none of this is sounding very positive," I said.

"But unlikely."

"So, what should I do now? I don't want to cause undue trouble, but by the same token, I don't want to be grounded for the rest of forever, either."

"I think it's probably best you just listen to Vincent for now," Sonny said. "You know, just do what he says."

"And why should I do that?"

"Because he cares about your wellbeing and wants you to be safe."

I scoffed. "Yeah, right. Are we forgetting the whole stab Clarissa in the heart and kill her in front of all the Patrons fiasco?" I asked, frowning at him.

"Hardly. It was one of my finest moments." He grinned.

I smacked him playfully and giggled when he winced.

"Easy," he said, rubbing his chest. "That hurt!"

"Oh, please." I rolled my eyes. "Big, tough man like you."

"Yeah, well, you're much stronger than you realize," he said, pulling the neck of his shirt down and examining his chest—his smooth, muscular, utterly perfect chest. "I think that's going to leave a bruise. Look." He pointed to his bare flesh and I swear my throat completely seized up.

"Look," he repeated. "Bruise."

I swallowed and looked everywhere except the patch of flesh where he was pointing.

"Oh, for heaven's sake, if I knew you were going to be such a baby about it."

Sonny looked at his watch and whistled. "Whoa, it's getting late. I better get going, hey?" He drained his second glass of Glenlivet.

Well that was sudden.

"Oh, okay," I said. "You know you don't have to—"

Sonny stood and grabbed his jacket from one of the coat hooks that hung in the hallway.

"—hurry off. Alrighty, then," I said, standing. "Quick exit."

"I've got to get some shut eye. Plenty to be done tomorrow if we've got any chance of finding Silvio alive."

"Of course. I mean, if you don't work out who's behind the kidnappings, there'll be no De Benedettos left."

His brow creased. "Yes."

I walked him to the door and stood awkwardly while he pulled on his jacket.

He paused and looked down at me.

"I know this is tough on you," he said. "But please try to keep a low profile, okay?" He brushed a stray hair behind my ear. "Which means stay here."

"Got it." I nodded.

"And if you're going to the cathedral, call ahead."

"Will do."

"And no more lunches at The Pantry, okay?"

I pulled back. "Are you stalking me?"

"Eyes and ears everywhere, Clarissa. Eyes and ears."

I should have known.

Sonny placed his hand on my cheek, and traced my jaw with his thumb, which sent the most delicious shivers skittering through every nerve in my body. Blood thundered through my veins, and waves of excitement fanned out from every spot his skin connected with mine.

Was this it? Was he going to kiss me? Finally? The anticipation was killing me. KILLING ME.

Slowly, Sonny lifted my hand to his mouth and pressed his lips gently to my palm. It was such a sweet gesture, I had to fight the urge to whimper from the sheer delight of it.

That's when he leaned back, breaking contact, and for a moment I wanted to screech at him and demand he put his hands back on me. But then his gaze dropped to my lips, and suddenly his palms weren't the only parts of his body I wanted to be connected to.

I gave myself a mental shake.

One step at a time, Clarissa.

And the first step was this kiss.

I blinked up at his ridiculously luminescent green eyes and could see the need simmering behind them. I wondered if he could see the same reflected in mine.

His lips parted ever so slightly, and his tongue darted out, sweeping over his lips. When I responded with a quiet sigh and mirrored his action, I heard the satisfying catch of his breath.

This *was* it.

This was actually *IT*!

He was going to kiss me.

He was going to kiss me.

He was going to…take a step backward and drop my hand like it was covered in herpes.

"Donatella," he whispered.

It was like being doused by a fire hose.

"No. I'm Clarissa, but clearly you wish I *was* Donatella."

"Max."

"What?"

"Donatella…"

"I told you, I'm —"

"… and Max. They're in danger."

"What? How do you know?"

"You just said so."

What? "Ah, I'm pretty sure I didn't—"

"If I don't work out who's behind the kidnappings, there'll be no De Benedettos left. You literally just said that."

I paused. "Well, I guess—"

"I could kiss you!"

DON'T LET ME STOP YOU!

"Gotta go, though. Sit tight. I'll be in touch," he said, disappearing out my front door and leaving me standing there, gaping like a demented goldfish.

"Wow, that was humiliating," Poppy said, materializing next to me, and shaking her head.

I couldn't speak.

Wait, what in the hell just happened?

Where the hell had he gone?

AND WHERE WAS MY GODDAMN KISS?

I had *no idea* what was going on and certainly had no clue what I'd said to make Sonny think Max and Donatella were in danger.

"Maybe I did something wrong?" I wondered.

"I don't think so," Poppy replied.

"Maybe I smell funky?" I raised my hand to my mouth and cupped it as I puffed warm breath into my palm and inhaled. "Oh, God," I groaned. "Garlic. I smell like garlic and I'm too gross to kiss."

I slumped a little.

Poppy stepped forward and sniffed me. "Actually, you smell like…like, pineapple."

"Pineapple? Better than garlic, I guess."

I trudged back to the couch to finish my drink. My self-esteem had taken a hit, a Donatella-sized hit, and finishing my whiskey seemed exactly the right way to boost my morale…and drown my sorrows. Either way, I was getting drunk, drunkity, drunk, drunk before I hit the sheets.

"You don't really think he's sleeping with Donatella, do you?" Poppy asked as she plonked herself down next to me on the couch.

I shot her a little, *you're kidding, right?* glare. "You think he's not?"

"I don't know. I kind of got the impression he was into you."

"That's because you haven't seen Donatella. She's like a goddess."

"I thought she was a werewolf?" Poppy said.

"She's a figurative goddess. She looks like she fell out of *Vogue* and I look like a rough sketch Pixar rejected."

I sighed and took another sip of my whiskey, but I'd lost the taste for it. So much for drowning my sorrows.

"I think you're beautiful," Poppy said.

I snorted, thankful I'd already swallowed the whiskey

because it would have burned like hot tea coming out my nose. "Of course you think I'm beautiful. We're twins."

She shot me a little eye roll. "That's beside the point."

I shook my head and we sat in silence for a few moments. I was actually waiting for her to start yammering on about one of the Real Housewives, but she stayed conspicuously quiet.

"Don't you have an episode of *Selling Sunset* to watch?"

When she didn't answer, I turned and looked at her. She had her pouty face on.

"What's the matter?" I asked.

"Nothing."

More pouty face.

"I don't have time for this," I said, crossing my arms over my chest. "Either tell me what's wrong or let me get on with my sulking."

Poppy sighed. "Why are you always so mean to me?"

Oh no. She was angling for a deep and meaningful conversation and I had the emotional energy of a porcupine—short and prickly.

"Mean to you? What are you even talking about?" I asked.

I knew exactly what she was talking about.

"I've missed you so much. Every single day we were apart, I wished… I *prayed* there was a way I could talk to you, laugh with you, and share secrets just like we did before I…um. Before I—"

"Before you up and died on me?" I snapped.

"You make it sound like I did it on purpose."

"You did. You gave up." My rational brain was screaming at me to *shut up*, but my fragile, emotional side had taken control of the ship and was sailing us straight into a shit storm.

"*What*? You think I died intentionally? You think I wanted to die?" Poppy shrieked. It made me wince.

I threw my hands in the air. "Intentional. Unintentional. Does it matter? You left me!"

Wow. This conversation was escalating quickly, and apparently, I'd tapped into some stuff I thought I'd resolved years ago. Dr. Huon was going to get a stern email from me in the morning, demanding a refund.

"I left you? I *LEFT* you? Of all the selfish, coldhearted, mind-numbingly egocentric things you could ever say." Poppy stood and paced the room. And when I say paced, I mean glided. Or was it glud? I still couldn't decide.

"Egocent—"

"I'm the one who died. You got to live and experience everything. You got to go to university. You got to experience friendships and sex and love and hate. And you got to do it while you were healthy! But you're shitty because I *left you?*"

"Well, when you put it that way—"

"At least it explains why you've been such a cow."

"*Cow*? Are you kidding me?" Now it was my turn to fire back. "I feed you. Constantly. I opened my home to you. I gave you your own room—"

"Oh, of course that's what you'd focus on. *Things.* You forget that you've told me to shut up or get out or go away every single day since—" She sniffled and I saw the first trickle of tears roll down her face which, in turn, almost instantly reduced *me* to tears.

Well done, Clarissa. Outstanding work.

"I guess I always thought you'd be happy to have me back," she snuffled.

My heart contracted, the ache radiating through my entire body. What a bitch I'd been. A heartless, selfish, well…bitch. There just wasn't any other word for it.

But how could I even begin to explain the reason behind my cold, oftentimes cruel behavior? I had to try.

"Of course, I'm happy you're back, Pops," I whispered.

"You've got a weird way of showing it," she shot back.

"You've been acting like it's torture having me back in your life."

I patted the couch next to me and without hesitation, she floated back over and flopped down. I sighed. "Because having you back has been torture."

Poppy turned her head and gave me her A-grade puppy-dog eyes. "Wow, *seriously*? You couldn't try to be a little more, I don't know, tactful? Try a little sensitivity, maybe?"

"Hey, you wanted the heart-to-heart." I shrugged. "I'm merely along for the ride. Plus, you know I'm a crappy liar." I closed my eyes and took a deep breath. "Having you back has been the best and worst thing that's ever happened to me."

"Pardon?"

"But that doesn't mean I'm not happy you're back. But it's a lot, you know?"

Poppy screwed her nose up, which usually meant she was either going to sneeze one of her giant sneezes that I'm pretty sure registered on the Richter Scale, or she was going to concede. I was hoping for the latter.

"I guess," she conceded.

Yes! Latter for the win.

"There are so many things I have to deal with right now, everything, I mean *everything* is different," I said. "And then you just magically reappear, and believe me when I say, I never imagined seeing you again, much less talking to you. I wasn't prepared. And you just keep popping in and out, which startles the pee out of me every time, and then I end up all edgy and neurotic. And then I get snappy. And you're always all up in my business and eating my snacks—" I pointed at the empty Doritos bag that she'd left on the coffee table. "See?"

"This is the worst pep talk ever," she said, and I snort-laughed before taking her hand and squeezing gently.

"I'm sorry I've been such a douche," I said. "You don't deserve that."

She squeezed my hand back. "I really don't."

"I just need more time. I have to be sure—" My throat tightened, strangling the words before I even had the chance to utter them.

"Sure of what?" Poppy asked, concern marring her pretty little face.

I cleared my throat. "I have to be sure you're back for good. That this is a forever thing, you know?"

She tilted her head like a confused Daschund and frowned. I hadn't seen that expression in over a decade. It made my heart glow.

"I need to know this is permanent and not just some glitch in the universe that'll wipe you out of my life again once I get to the bottom of this werewolf heart business." I shook my head.

"You've been keeping me at a distance, so you don't get attached?"

I nodded. "Because I just don't think I could go through it again."

"Through what?" she asked.

"Losing you. Once was hard enough," I admitted. "One more time and I'm not sure I—"

Poppy squeezed my hand harder. "You don't have to worry," she placated. "I'm not going anywhere."

I turned and searched her face. I knew every inch of it intimately, every freckle, every laugh line. I could pick up if she was lying in an instant.

She wasn't lying.

"Seriously. This is me, here for good. Forever."

"Promise?" I asked.

She nodded. "Cross my heart."

FOUR

"WILL YOU STOP PACING, PLEASE? You're making me dizzy," Vincent said, taking a giant swig from an elegant crystal glass. I think he was drinking brandy, or it could have been ginger ale, I had no idea.

"I can't stop. I'm too nervous. In just..." I glanced at my phone. "...two hours, it's going to be sunset. *Sunset*!"

"Yes, I'm aware of that," Vincent said, refilling his glass with amber liquid and dropping a couple of ice cubes in it.

"And it's the full mooooon."

"Yes, I'm aware of that, too. What I don't understand is why you're here, wearing out my Ziegler Mahal rug, and yammering on about it."

Sonny stepped into Vincent's office and closed the door behind him. I hadn't seen him since the humiliating almost-kissy episode—five whole days. It's the longest I'd gone without seeing him since the day he insinuated himself into my life, and I hadn't missed him at all. I presumed he'd been hanging out with Donatella, taking care of Inner World business that didn't concern me. Or they could have been bumping uglies for all I knew. But I was not at all jealous. Not even a smidge.

#liar

#shutupinnerself

"She's worried she's going to sprout claws and fangs, and get all bitey," Sonny said, shooting me a lopsided grin.

"Yes, but why is she doing it here?" Vincent asked.

"You don't know. I might!" I said, wondering why I seemed to be the only one bothered by this. I was also wondering where he'd been for nearly a week, but I had more pressing issues to deal with, like my imminent attack of lycanthropy.

"You won't," Sonny placated. "At least I don't think you will." He too poured himself a drink from the cut glass decanter and joined Vincent on the couch.

"But what if I do? I only had my nails done last week...and my highlights. Miss Lisa is going to have a shitfit." I glanced at my pretty pink nails and imagined how terrible they were going to look after I wolfed out. "This is just the worst." I flopped down on the chaise longue and sighed. "And it's all your fault," I said, glaring at Sonny.

"How is this my fault?" he asked, throwing his hands in the air.

"I'm not sure. Maybe because you've been off doing God knows what for the past week instead of paying attention to what's happening with me."

Sonny cocked his head and squinted at me.

"And now I have the pleasure of hearing you freak out about it for the rest of the night, do I?" Vincent said. "Aren't I lucky?"

"Freak out?" I said, raising my brows.

"Yes, well, perhaps I'm spending too much time with you."

"No perhaps about it," I replied.

"But I do have an idea that will fix the problem," Vincent said.

"And what's that?"

"I think Sonny should be the one to babysit you for the evening."

"And how exactly does that fix the problem?" Sonny asked.

"Apologies. I should rephrase, it fixes *my* problem."

"I don't need babysitting," I said.

"Of course you do," Vincent replied. "To ensure you don't wolf-out and tear up some poor homeless guy. Like that time with Sergi and...well, you remember the unpleasantness."

Both Vincent and Sonny shuddered, which can I say, was more than a little disturbing. When the things that rule the other things that go bump in the night get weirded out, you just know it's going to be a really gross story.

"Who's Sergi?" I asked, and immediately regretted the question. "You know what, I don't want to know. This just sucks beyond the telling of it and I'm absolutely not going to be babysat by this...this...butt wipe."

I knew I'd regressed into adolescent name calling, but he was a butt wipe. He'd been off fraternizing with a werewolf floozy and shirking his Peacekeeping responsibilities. I had every right to call him names, or at least I would have if we'd been in an actual relationship that extended beyond vague flirting and the odd X-rated dream. On my part, that is.

"Who you calling a butt wipe?"

"You, that's who," I replied.

"Okay, enough," Vincent said, standing abruptly. "Both of you shut up."

Vincent scrubbed his hands over his face and sighed. "You two make my head spin. It's like dog-sitting two yappy Pomeranians. It never stops! Yap, yap, yap. All the damn time and I've just about had enough."

"He started it," I said, then regretted it almost immediately when Vincent sneered at me.

"So, here's what's going to happen. Sonny, you are going to take Clarissa to your place, or her place, or any place that *isn't here*, and you will watch her, and, if she should happen to turn into a werewolf, you will make sure that she doesn't eat anyone's face off."

"You can't make me... I'm not going anywhere with him. I—"

"Shoosh!" Vincent said, slicing his hand through the air in front of my face like a maestro. "Just, be quiet," he said, turning to Sonny. "Just, get her the hell out of here."

Sonny's face sank. "But—"

"I said out!" Vincent yelled, pointing to the door. "*Noooow.*"

Both Sonny and I scrambled to our feet, collected our belongings, and hustled out the door. For the most part, Vincent was nice and all, but when he was angry, like for real angry, he was like, *yikes*!

FIVE

IT WAS A MISTAKE GOING TO SONNY'S PLACE instead of mine. My place was cozy and warm and overlooked a lake. Sonny's place was dark and sparse and smelled like gunpowder and knife oil.

"You want something to eat?" he called from the kitchen. I was in the lounge, looking through his record collection, and yes, I do mean actual records—as in vinyl LPs. And not the new ones that were making a comeback. Nope. I'm talking old school, original pressings—some dating back to the 50s and 60s. They would have been worth a small fortune.

"See anything you like?" Sonny asked, startling me, as usual. I never heard him when he approached. I mean, I knew his stealth game was impeccable, but it was really taking its toll on my nerves.

"I'm going to put a bell around your neck," I said, pushing him aside. "You're so damn quiet."

"What can I say, it's a skill." He shrugged. "Now, did you want something to eat or not? Can I tempt you with a small child? Or a pint of blood from a nubile virgin? Something befitting a new lycanthrope."

"Oh, my God! What's wrong with you?"

"I'm kidding. Relax. There's leftover pizza or I have cold cuts."

"No, thank you. I'm fine. I'm really not hungry." I went back to perusing his LPs.

Who the hell could even think about food at a time like this? Sonny, that's who.

"So, which is your favorite?" I asked, pointing at the records in a vain attempt at distracting myself.

"Zeppelin, Sabbath, Maiden," he said, pulling a record from the collection and placing it on the turntable. Screeching guitars blasted from the speakers hidden in the cabinetry, and the windows rattled.

I picked up the album sleeve and studied the intricate cover art. *Powerslave*. "You a big Led Zeppelin fan?"

"Actually, I am. Of course, this is Iron Maiden," he corrected, taking the album cover from me and placing it on a small stand next to the turntable.

"You know what? I don't even care," I said, feeling quite defeated and uncharacteristically restless. "Sorry."

I was beginning to feel hot, like from the inside out. My skin was tingling and I felt squirmy and fidgety. Something was definitely happening to me. I'd seen *An American Werewolf in London*. I knew the pending doom of transformation when I saw it, or in this case, felt it. I was going to bloody well turn into a drooly, stinky werewolf and there was zippo I could do about it.

"So, you know Beverley, the werewolf I, um, you know—"

"Ripped apart with your bare hands?" Sonny said, chewing on a cold piece of pizza.

"Must you always?"

He nodded and grinned wildly. "Yup!"

"Yeah, well, I wish you'd stop it. I'm freaking out here!"

There it was, that high and whiny tone I'd taken to using so frequently.

I felt the well of hot tears prick the backs of my eyes, and my nose started running. Oh, how attractive I must have looked.

"Shit, you're serious?" Sonny said, putting his pizza down on the coffee table, crossing the room and taking me by the hands. "I'm sorry. I didn't mean—I'm just trying to distract you, so you don't lose your mind and get all, well, Clarissa on me."

"Well, it's not working." I sniffled, angry at myself for crying in front of Sonny. That's all he needed, more fodder for his smarmy sarcasm and incessant mocking. "And what exactly do you mean by, 'getting all Clarissa on you?'"

"You know…this." He waggled his fingers in front of my face. "All high strung and shrieky."

Which made me cry more.

"I'm an idiot," Sonny said, softy. "What can I do to make you feel better?"

Take your clothes off and do a sexy dance?

Whoa! I paused for a moment, not entirely sure whether I'd said it out loud or had the good sense to keep it as part of my internal monologue.

He didn't respond, didn't react in any way, so I was pretty sure I hadn't said it out loud. *Phew*! Internal monologue for the win.

Sonny was peering at me, though, and I realized he was waiting for an answer to his question. Which was…? Um… *What can I do to make you feel better?* I think. Visions of the sexy dance filled my head again. I was definitely losing it.

"Nothing," I mumbled, mainly because I didn't trust myself to not say anything stupid. "Because I'm going to transform into something horrendous and probably tear up your beautiful apartment."

"Relax," he soothed. "You're not going to transform into anything. At most, you might develop another werewolf trait and that'll be it." He drew me close, wrapped his arms around me and rested his chin on the top of my head.

I breathed in and his scent enveloped me, like sunshine and rain and wet earth. I pulled away from him slightly and looked up into his dreamy green eyes.

"What kind of trait?" I breathed.

"Sorry?"

"What kind of werewolfy trait do you think I could develop?" I asked.

"Well, I'm not sure—"

"*Ohmygod*, I'm not going to sprout a tail, am I?"

Panic. Rising.

Urgh.

"I wouldn't think so, no," he replied.

"Well, *what then*?"

"I guess that really depends on what species of werewolf heart was transplanted into you," he said. "They're all a bit different."

"But we don't know what type of werewolf it was." I drooped.

"No, we don't. But there are some traits that are universal."

"Like?"

"Well, there's super strength," he said.

"I think I've already got that covered."

"True. Okay, there's accelerated healing, which you also have already," Sonny said. "Heightened sense of smell, hearing, agility, but you've got those, too."

"This is terrible," I said, pulling away and stalking to the window. The sun was setting, and it was only a matter of minutes before I was going to wolf-out and bid bye-bye to my normal life, which really wasn't all that normal anymore. But still, it wasn't howl-at-the-moon batshit crazy, either.

"Oooh! I know!" Sonny said, snapping his fingers. "Got it!

Werewolves are highly, err—" He stopped mid-sentence and averted his eyes.

Okay, what was that about? What could possibly be that bad that it actually rendered him speechless?

"Werewolves are highly what?" I asked, loosening my shirt and rubbing the back of my neck to ease some of the tension that was coiling through my body.

I fanned myself with both hands. "Is it getting hot in here?" I asked. "Seriously, I'm burning up."

There was also a peculiar tingling sensation skittering through my body and settling in the most inconvenient place... right between my legs. Truth be told, the feeling was driving me a little crazy, but I wasn't about to tell Sonny that.

"Are you okay?" Sonny asked, eying me warily.

"Huh? Yeah, I'm fine. I'm just hot. Are you hot? I mean, of course you're hot. You're just about the hottest thing I've ever clapped eyes on."

Sonny's eyes widened, transforming him into six-feet-four-inches of stunned sinew and adorable freckles.

Welp that obviously bypassed my internal monologue and went straight to the foot-in-mouth part of the tour. What the hell had gotten into me? I was eyeing him like he was a juicy steak and I hadn't eaten in a month. I had to get a grip.

"What were you saying?" I asked, clearing my throat. "About the werewolves. You thought of another trait."

"Well, it's not so much a trait as it is, um...a characteristic."

"What the hell does that even mean? Characteristic? What type of characteristic?"

"They, um..."

"Oh for pity's sake, man, just spit it out."

He stepped back and took a deep breath. "Okay, so were-wolves are breeders. Big-time breeders. They're are renowned for their heightened sex drives and their insatiable, er, appetites."

Um, what?

"And when you say appetites, you wouldn't happen to be referring to pigging out at the Taco Bell all-you-can-eat enchilada buffet, would you?"

He shook his head. "No. They're pretty much sex-machines."

I threw my head back and whined. "Are you kidding me? Because if you are, it's really not funny."

"I'm really not."

This was noooooooot good.

"So, the sun goes down and I'm going to, what, turn into a raging were-slut?"

"I wouldn't say were-*slut* is the appropriate term, Clarissa. I mean it's perfectly healthy for females, human or otherwise, to express their sexuality whichever way they choose—"

"Yes, yes I know," I snapped. "Slut-shaming is a very bad thing, but this is neither the time nor place for political correctness, Sonny," I barked. "Any minute now I'm going to start having sex with... With the first...hot-bodied..." I eyed him hungrily. Was he always this sexy? I mean, I knew he was sexy, but wow. "... long-haired, well-muscled man to cross my path?"

"Well, I wouldn't exactly say that."

"Because," I said, taking slow steady steps toward him. "If that's the case, I think maybe—"

Sonny put his hands out as if to ward me off. "Stop. Whatever you're about to say, no good can come if it."

"I don't know," I cooed, closing the gap between us. When he finally bumped into the wall behind him, I grinned. "I think something really, really good, could...come, you know?"

I couldn't help but notice how his pupils dilated and his breath came in short, shallow bursts. If I didn't know better, I would say he was experiencing a little spike in his own sexual appetite.

And I was planning to take full advantage of it.

"Listen, I don't know what's going on, but I think you should probably back up," Sonny croaked.

"What's the matter? You feeling a little intimidated? Afraid you won't be able to perform?"

"Oh, I can perform, Clarissa. I can *always* perform."

"So, what's the hesitation? Is it Donatella?"

"Huh? What's she got to do with it?"

"It's obvious you're not interested in me, so I assume that's because you're with her."

"What? No. Why would you even say that?"

"So, you're not with her, then?" I asked.

"No. Of course not."

"Then why aren't you interested in me?"

"Who says I'm not?"

"Interesting," I purred, inching closer to him. I felt emboldened. I felt sexy. I felt *alive*. "You've never made a move. I would have thought you might have by now. If you were genuinely interested, that is."

"Because, *oh God*—" His words dissolved into nothing more than breathy groans when I scraped my nails gently down his chest and placed a slow, wet kiss at the base of his throat. He tasted so sweet, like honey and molasses. "Stop that. Stop that, now."

"Why?" I said, undoing the first of the buttons on the front of my shirt.

"Good question," he said. "Very good question." He cleared his throat. "Oh, I remember. Because I'm not the kind of man who takes advantage of someone who—"

"Takes advantage? Ha! You wouldn't be taking anything I wasn't already planning to give you," I cooed.

"Clarissa, you're not yourself. That's obvious. The sun has gone down—"

I licked my lips.

"Okay, bad choice of words. The sun has set, and it's a full moon... Hey, look!" He pointed out the window. "You didn't turn into a werewolf. That's great, isn't it?" The usual low timbre of his voice had been replaced by this sort of squeaky pitch you'd more likely hear from a teenage boy than a centuries-old, er... whatever he was.

I glared at him. "But?"

"But I'm pretty sure you've just gone into heat and this—" He pointed to himself, then to me, then back to himself. "This isn't a good idea."

"Why not?"

"Well, firstly, you hate me."

"Hate is an awfully strong word, Sonny," I said, slipping my shirt off my shoulders and flinging it across the room. His breath caught at the sight of the gorgeous, white-lace bra I'd put on that morning. I grinned in satisfaction. It felt nice to be desired.

And I knew one hundred percent that he wanted me. I could smell the lust radiating off his body like a beacon. It was woodsy, with undertones of vanilla, cinnamon, and peppermint. It was delightful and delicious.

"Yeah, well, you've used it often enough," he said with a gulp. "I think you tell me you hate me at least once a day."

"Think of it as foreplay," I said, reaching for the button on my jeans and popping it open.

"We clearly have different ideas of what can be classified as foreplay," he said, unable to take his eyes off my heaving chest.

"Well, why don't you educate me?" I said, sliding my jeans down my legs and stepping out of them.

Sonny didn't know where to look. I mean, I knew where he wanted to look, but he was being all gentlemanly about it, which was kind of cute, but also kind of annoying.

"Listen, Clarissa, we can't do this."

"Oh, but I think we can. In fact, I know we can."

"You don't understand. There's something you don't know about werewolves when they mate."

"But I'm not a werewolf."

"Part of you is. A very important part."

"Okay, I'll play along. This thing I don't know about when werewolves mate, does it involve me killing you afterward?" I asked.

"You're already killing me," he said.

I smiled. "I mean, *actually* killing you. Like a female praying mantis?"

"No. It's not that. It's—"

I placed the tip of my index finger on his lips, which silenced him immediately. "Then I don't care what it is. All I care about is finding out what you've got hiding in those tight jeans of yours."

I reached out and unfastened his button fly (PS: was Levi Strauss some kind of sadist? Who in their right mind thought *this* many buttons on a pair of pants was a good idea?) and traced the inside of the waistband with the tips of my fingers.

I noted that while he'd stiffened, and I do mean, *stiffened*, he didn't fend me off.

Good sign.

"Clarissa," Sonny said my name on a sigh.

"Yes?" I replied, reaching farther into his jeans, and wrapping my hand around his—*oh, my*. Thank you, whoever created this little slice of yumminess.

"Never mind," Sonny said, pushing himself into my hand and fisting my hair. He yanked my head back, his lips feathering mine. He stood there, looking directly in my eyes for a few seconds and then let out a guttural growl before plundering my mouth with his.

So, as the final rays of daylight slipped below the horizon, Sonny and I melted into a hot, needy pool of sweat and sex.

And then everything went black.

SIX

I WOKE UP to a spear of sunlight shining on my face and a kink knotting up my neck.

My head hurt, my mouth was dry and parts of me were very…tender. It felt like I'd spent the night riding a mechanical bull, only I couldn't remember going to the Moon Dog Brewery, and I didn't know of any other places in Melbourne where they actually had mechanical bulls.

Truth was, I couldn't remember a lot about the previous night, or day for that matter.

I stretched my arms above my head and yawned, blinking at the morning sun and slowly looked around the room. Three enormous black-and-white photos hung on the wall opposite the bed. They featured magnificent cityscapes of Paris, New York, and Rome. They were grainy and artsy and really quite beautiful in a melancholy way. Not at all my usual style.

When in the hell had I gotten those?

As my mind slowly defogged, it dawned on me that there was something very, very wrong with my bedroom. I took further stock of what was around me. Heavy, dark wood furniture, rich velvet blackout drapes, king-size mahogany sleigh bed.

I felt like I was living in a Talking Heads song.

This is not my beautiful bed.

This is not my beautiful life.

Oh. Dear. Lord.

It was Sonny's bed.

I was in Sonny's bed!

How???

I rubbed my eyes with the heels of my hands and tried to think back to the night before.

What in the hell had happened?

I remembered Vincent kicking me out of his office and ordering Sonny to babysit me, much to my chagrin. I remembered arguing with Sonny about…pizza, maybe? And listening to some screechy guitar music as the sun set across the Melbourne skyline.

I remembered Sonny hugging me and saying the sweetest things to me—although that could very easily have been a dream. It was unlikely he'd actually been sweet to me. He usually treated me like I was his comedy relief.

That's when it all started coming back. I remembered feeling, let's call it amorous, thinking I might just explode if I didn't get some kind of release.

Flashes of taking off my shirt and jeans came flooding back. It was a little hazy but I remembered throwing myself at Sonny. I remembered gnashing teeth and tangling tongues, upturning furniture, sweat-slicked skin. I remembered Sonny picking me up and carrying me to his bed.

That's when the rubbing started.

OH MY GOD! SO MUCH RUBBING!

I clutched the rumpled bed sheet covering my body, then bracing myself, quickly pulled it away and looked down.

Yep.

I was naked.

Bare-assed naked, like the day I was born.

A quick glance around the room revealed a scene straight out of *Hansel and Gretel*... If Hansel and Gretel were lurid perverts.

Instead of breadcrumbs, we'd left a trail of clothes strewn behind us, starting with Sonny's Doc Martens flung haphazardly in the doorway and ending all the way across the room at the foot of the bed where I spied... Wait, were they? Yep, they were.

My balled-up panties.

Oh, for fuc—

"Penny for your thoughts."

I shrieked and snapped my head to the left to find Sonny's emerald gaze fixed on me.

"You're a little jumpy this morning," he said, cocking his brow. "Something wrong?"

My gaze—dirty little slut that it was—slid down his body. His perfectly chiseled chest was bare, save for a smattering of hair that was just begging to be stroked. His lower half covered only by the crumpled sheet we were sharing.

His right hand was behind his head, and his left was splayed across his belly. He couldn't have looked hotter if he tried.

Stupid, hot, stupid Sonny.

"What the hell did you do to me last night, you...you—*Neanderthal*?" I growled.

Sonny shook his head, a lazy smile tugging at the corners of his lips. "I should be asking you that question. As I recall, you were the one getting all up in my stuff—"

I raised my hand. "Stop. Please don't. I don't want to hear about what I did to your stuff." Humiliation flooded my cheeks. "I know I may have tried to...instigate..."

"Instigate what?" he prodded.

I groaned. "Relations."

"Whatever do you mean?" he asked.

"You know exactly what I mean."

"Yeah, but I just want to hear you say it."

"A gentleman wouldn't—"

He threw his head back and laughed before lacing both hands behind his head. "Baby, I'm no gentleman." The sheet covering his man-bits—his gloriously substantial man-bits—slipped lower.

"You can say that again," I mumbled, forcing myself to look away.

"Besides," he said, shifting so the sheet inched even lower.

The bastard. He knew I couldn't help but look.

"No one, not in their right mind, anyway, has the power to resist you, Clarissa."

I wanted to tell him he was delusional, that a real gentleman could have, nay *would* have, resisted my advances because I clearly wasn't of sound mind, but all I could think about was ripping the damn bed sheet off his toned body and reliving some of our sexcapades from the night before.

I'd completely thrown myself at him. I'd been all sloppy, and panty, and drooly, practically dry humping his leg right in the middle of his lounge room, damn it.

"Still, you could have done something," I whined.

"Oh, I did something—"

"Something to stop me!" I clarified.

He baulked. "Not a chance."

"Please, just stop," I groaned, pulling the sheet up tight under my chin.

"Not that I blame you," he continued, turning his wicked grin toward me. "I mean, who wouldn't want to get with this?" He gestured to his abs. His deeply ridged, rock-hard abs that I wanted to do body shots off. "You know I've got what you need."

"You're revolting," I said.

"With all due respect, I'm not the one who said she wanted to... What was it? Oh yes, you said you were going to ride me until my knees buckled and I forgot my own name, which, I'm pleased to report, you did with great success."

"Will you please just shut up?" I begged. "I didn't... I mean, I wasn't... My God, the groping. There was so much groping," I said.

"There was licking, too," he added.

"Why couldn't you just stop me?"

"Oh, come on. I'm only human," he said.

"*No, you're not!* I don't even know *what* you are! What kind of a person has crazy monkey sex with someone without even knowing what *species* they are?"

This had to have something to do with my werewolf heart. It was wreaking havoc on my body.

"I'm so embarrassed I could die."

"Clarissa, you have *nothing* to be embarrassed about. Trust me," he consoled.

I didn't respond, just tried to keep my eyes straight ahead and focused on the giant photos.

"You know what?" Sonny said, glancing at his wristwatch and flinging the sheet away without so much as a word of warning. "As much fun as dissecting your sexual hang-ups has been, I have somewhere to be this morning. Sooooo..." He sat up on the side of the bed and stretched his impressive arms over his head. Then, sweet baby Jesus, he stood, affording me an unobstructed view of his oh-so-perfect butt, which looked just like a ripe peach—smooth, tight, and very bitable. It was the best damn tushy I'd seen since the *ManPower* All-Male Review my cousins Cristina, Sabrina, and I went to for my twenty-first, and it was all I could do to stop myself from reaching out and giving it a little squeeze.

"See something you like?"

I glanced up to find his eyes pinned to mine, a slow, sexy grin spreading across his face.

"Don't be ridiculous," I spluttered. "I just wish you'd cover up your...your..." I was pointing in the direction of his butt.

"You know, if my ass offends, I could always give you an eyeful of something else." He turned slowly, the view of his pert keester giving way to his splendid, erm... Well, not his keester.

"Stop," I said, trying, with only moderate success, not to ogle him. "Please, just put something on." My protests might have been more convincing if I'd turned away or closed my eyes or blushed or did *ANYTHING* other than just *gawk* at him like some sex-starved maven. I'm pretty sure, at one point, my mouth watered. It actually *watered*.

"Little late to be getting prudish, pet," Sonny cooed. "Not after all the dirty little words you whispered in my ear last night. All those breathy moans..."

There was the damn tingling again, and the X-Rated flashbacks.

This werewolf heart was killing me, and if it didn't finish me off, Sonny definitely would. He was just sooooo damn impressive—from the top of his shaggy head, to the tips of his toes, and every tasty, tanned, toned inch in between, he was pretty much, well, perfect.

Sonny bent down and grabbed the sheet covering me, and yanked on it. Hard.

One minute, I was like a giant sushi roll wrapped up and snug in the sheet, and the next, I was spinning through the air like an amateur acrobat auditioning for Cirque du Soleil.

"Heeeeey!" I shrieked, landing with a none-too-elegant thud on the wooden floor with all my stuff out for everyone to see. Sonny gave me a little once-over, smiled appreciatively, and wrapped the sheet around his waist

"I'll be taking a shower," he said, turning toward what I presume was the en suite. "Just in case you feel like joining me."

I surged to my feet, took two steps forward and stomped on the sheet that billowed behind him like a glorious peacock tail.

He stopped with a jerk and turned to face me, his broad chest flexing as he crossed his arms.

His amazingly green eyes darkened, and his body thickened as his eyes drifted lazily over me. It was no quick once-over this time. This time, his gaze lingered on all my private bits (which weren't exactly private anymore) and I felt the air go static around us, crackling and snapping.

"I was using that," I croaked, pointing to the sheet.

He laughed and I watched, utterly hypnotized as his hands dropped to his waist and his fingers played with the sheet that was slung so very, very low on his hips. Splaying his hand on his abdomen, Sonny loosened the satin, and edged his fingers downward.

Down.

Down.

Down.

Stopping only when his fingertips dipped below the sheet.

"You sure you want this back, pet?" he purred.

"Huh?" I said.

"Are you sure you want the sheet back?"

What the hell was he talking about? I regained my senses enough to respond and nodded defiantly. "Yes."

He obliged, unwrapping himself and walking toward me, every inch of his silky-smooth, rigid body on display for me to enjoy.

Just for me.

Only me.

Mine.

Forever.

And ever.

Whoa-ho-ho. Where the hell had that come from?

Mine.

Forever.

And ever.

The words echoed in my head.

Sonny stopped when he was close enough for me to feel the heat radiating off him. He smelled of musk and sex and I couldn't place what else, but it was sweet and intoxicating and oh, so delicious. All I wanted to do was climb him like a tree and impale myself on him just one more time, because it would definitely be the last time. No way was I letting the previous evening's escapades happen again. Once was enough. Okay, it wasn't exactly once. It was many onces. But it would definitely, most probably, maybe never happen again.

Mine.

Forever.

And ever.

Oh, shut up, brain. You're sex addled and cock-struck. You have no idea what you're saying.

When I saw Sonny reach for me, I didn't pull away. I couldn't. I was ready to pop all over again, and all I wanted was for him to pop me.

He leaned forward, buried his head in my hair and inhaled deeply.

"I can smell myself all over you," he murmured, brushing his lips against my neck, then along my jaw. "Can you smell me?"

My throat contracted and my mouth went dry, which was a stunning contrast of what was happening to other parts of my body. I couldn't speak, I could hardly breathe, and all common sense had flown out the window. So, I nodded in agreement.

I could feel him smile against my collarbone. "Good," he whispered. "Better get used to it."

Everything inside me burst to life. EVERYTHING. Every millimeter of my body tingled and throbbed and when he groaned, I felt my knees give way.

The memories of the night before returned in long, languid waves. His hands touching me everywhere, his lips and tongue exploring, teasing, and playing. My body arching and stretching in response to his length, his width, eager, so very eager, for him to fill and coax me in a way I knew only he could.

I'd never had it so good; I knew that for certain. But I'm pretty sure he hadn't either.

Mine.

Forever.

And ever.

I became vaguely aware that Sonny had pulled away and was speaking to me.

"Wh-what?" I stammered, shaking off the sex-brain fog. "What did you say?"

"It's all yours," he repeated, and the right side of his mouth quirked.

"What is?" I asked. I'd clearly missed a significant part of the conversation

"The sheet." He was holding out the one-thousand-count Egyptian cotton bedding in front of me and gesturing for me to take it.

What in the hell was happening?

This wasn't the direction I hoped the morning would head. This was not the right direction at all!

Instead of taking the sheet, I simply stared at it. So, Sonny released it and we both watched as it floated to the floor and pooled like indigo silk around my feet.

And, without another word, he turned, walked into the en suite and slammed the door behind him.

What. The. Fuuu—

SEVEN

"HOW WAS YOUR NIGHT?" Poppy asked, floating through the wall into the bathroom and perching herself on the side of the tub I'd been soaking in for twenty minutes.

"What's that supposed to mean?" I asked, sinking deeper into the steaming water.

"Um, it's supposed to mean, how was your night?" She gently rapped her knuckles on the side of my head. "Did the full moon fry your brain?"

"Stop that," I said, swatting at her, sending tiny, foamy bubbles in all directions.

"So, did you wolf out? You know, grrrrr." Poppy curled her fingers to mimic gnarled claws and bared her teeth.

I rolled my eyes. "Not exactly," I replied, inhaling the heavenly scent of lemongrass and patchouli. I'd added bubbles to the water along with effervescent bath crystals; exactly what I needed to ease the sex aches from my body.

I felt my cheeks flush.

Sex aches.

Yummy, oh-so-satisfying, sex aches.

Oh, FFS.

Every time I thought about the previous night, more memories of Sonny and his magical mystery member came flooding back. I'd lost count how many times we'd had sex, or how many positions we'd done it in. There were a lot. The memories ran like constant, vivid movies—pornos if you will—in my head. They were so distracting. I'd almost driven off the road on the way home just thinking about the things he had done with—

"Cryptic, much?" Poppy continued, snapping me back to reality. "So, no tail? No fangs?"

"Nope. I'm pleased to report I'm a lycan-free zone."

She clapped her hands and did the little bouncing-on-the-spot thing she'd been doing since we were about four years old.

"That's good news, right?" she asked, noticing my lack of enthusiasm.

"Yep," I replied, flatter than a tack.

"Then why did you look happier when I broke your Bratz Doll?"

"Because I may have inherited a shiny new wolfie-trait that I now have to deal with every month."

"Oooh! Like a superpower?"

"Not exactly."

"It's not a mega-period, is it?" Poppy grimaced. "Because that would seriously suck."

"What? No. Where'd you even get that from?"

"You said you had to deal with it every month—"

"Because of the full moon, you nuffy, not because of my menstrual cycle."

"What then?" Her eyes were wide with anticipation.

After our little heart-to-heart, I'd been trying my hardest to stop pushing Poppy away. Truth was, though, I was still adjusting to having her around. They teach you all sorts of things at school. How to think independently, how to be resourceful and resilient… How to build a perfect replica of the solar system out of Styrofoam. But what they don't teach you is how to live with your twin sister's ghost—because it isn't as easy as you might think.

There was the obvious weirdness factor—we're talking ghosts after all—*but* in my case, we're talking about a ghost that looked exactly the way she had when she was fourteen, the age she died. Only, Poppy wasn't fourteen anymore, not mentally anyway. She was a full-grown woman, just like me. She had hopes and dreams, passions and peeves, thoughts and ideas well beyond what you'd expect from a kid.

Not to mention she had the attitude of a surly bartender, and the potty mouth to match.

I had to constantly remind myself that I was talking to a full-fledged adult cursed to spend eternity in a kid's body. Well, not a body, exactly. She was a ghost, after all. She had no body, per se. She had… What the hell were ghosts even made of? Seriously. I'm not kidding. I really wanted to know.

The whole situation reminded me of Claudia from *An Interview with the Vampire,* only Poppy didn't have crazy Shirley Temple hair or a penchant for hiding dead women in her bed.

I hoped.

"Well?" Poppy said, impatiently. "What is it then?"

"Okay, so it seems, every full moon, I'm…" I took a deep breath. "I'm going to go into heat and have sex with the first person I clap eyes on."

Poppy's brow furrowed. "That doesn't sound very much like a super-power. Are you sure?"

"Pretty sure."

"But how can you be *really* sure?"

"Because it happened last night."

This time, Poppy's brows shot up.

"You had sex last night?"

I nodded.

"With whom?"

"Who do you think?" My skin tingled at the mere thought of Sonny and his delightful tongue, gentle fingers, and magical mystery member.

"I'm sure I don't have a clue. Last I knew you were going to —*ohmygod*! You didn't have sex with Vincent, did you?"

"What? No. Why would you even say that?"

"Isn't that where you were headed yesterday afternoon?"

"Oh. Well, yes, but it wasn't Vincent. Sonny was there, too."

Her brows shot up even higher.

"You had sex with Sonny?"

I nodded.

"In front of Vincent?"

"*What*?"

"Oh, Clarissa." Poppy shook her head. "I try to be supportive. I try not to judge, I really do. But that's just—"

"No, dufus. We were at Sonny's place. Vincent sent us away because he said I was being all Clarissa—" I used air quotes when I said my own name.

"Screechy and neurotic?" Poppy asked.

I sighed and nodded. "And then, we were listening to Black Sabbath, or whatever, I don't remember exactly, and he was being all nice, and I was totally freaking out."

"No surprises there."

"Then the sun went down, and I may or may not have thrown myself at him."

"Really? This is so exciting!" She was happy clapping again. "You have to tell me e-v-e-r-y-t-h-i-n-g!"

"Firstly, quiet down. I don't want anyone else knowing what happened."

"Who the hell else is going to hear?" She looked around the empty bathroom and landed on the bottle of bubble bath I'd left in the vanity. "Mr. Matey?"

"Don't be daft. I was thinking more along the lines of Mrs. Brady from next door."

"You mean, she of the hearing aids and blaring TV? That woman's deaf as a post."

"And yet she knows every single thing that goes on around here. I'm pretty sure she's camped out at her front window, binoculars at the ready, 24/7."

"The Secret Service should seriously consider recruiting her as part of their surveillance team," Poppy said. "She's like the eyes and ears of the place."

"Right? She's a snooping machine. So please just keep it down. I don't want her telling everyone in the complex that I, you know, got jiggy wit' it, last night."

"Jiggy wit' it? Yeah, okay, Fresh Prince. You do know it's not 1997 anymore, right?"

I just glared at her. What would she even know? She was barely born in 1997.

"Okay, so I have to know, was it hot?" she continued, oblivious to the fact that I didn't really want to talk about it. "I bet it was amazing. He's built like a Greek god, isn't he?"

"Yes, yes, and yes," I groaned. "It was hot. It was all sorts of amazing. And yes, he's definitely built like a Greek god. No. He's better than a Greek god. He's—"

"Hemsworthy?"

I sighed. "Definitely."

"Then why do you look like someone stole your puppy?" she asked. "Shouldn't you be basking in the afterglow? What's with all the angst?"

"Because I slept with Sonny, and he's awful. He's arrogant. And sarcastic. He's a complete dick. He treats me like I'm a dimwit. He's totally disrespectful. I mean, he killed me, for heaven's sake and *WHY THE HELL CAN'T I STOP THINKING ABOUT HIM?*"

"Um, maybe because he's not awful at all? Maybe because

he's smart and brave and funny," Poppy cooed. "And he's been so sweet and tender lately—other than that time he killed you—but, you know, he's also extreeeemely nice to look at."

"You're not helping," I said, dropping a wet washcloth over my face and willing myself not to think about what it felt like to have Sonny's lips all over me.

"Well, I think you're overreacting."

Hmph. Easy for her to say.

●

"Clarissa didn't turn into a werewolf." Poppy beamed when Azrael sauntered through my front door, tossing his keys on the hall table and making a beeline for the fridge.

I swear that man was eating me out of house and home. My grocery bill had more than tripled since he poofed back into my life. At one point, I'd actually contemplated charging him board.

Ever since Sonny *killed* me, Azrael had been an even more regular presence in my life, especially after it came to light that killing me was actually a clever ruse devised to protect me from certain parties who wanted me dead. The result? Azrael now spent most of his evenings at my place, sprawled on my couch, eating my snacks, clogging my toilet (don't worry, I made him fix that!) and watching my Netflix.

I originally thought he felt guilty for letting me down, for not foreseeing what Sonny and Vincent had planned to do to me, and that he felt stupid for not realizing it was all for show.

But then I found out he was in on the whole plan, and he hadn't been out of the loop at all. That he was, in fact, a full member of #teamkillclarissabutnotreally

As I understood it, after Sonny told me the truth about his involvement in Kill Clarissa Gate, Azrael sought him out and beat the snot out of him. Apparently, he'd only agreed to participate in the plan with the caveat that I was never to find out Azrael had been involved.

Interestingly, though, there were no beatings for Vincent, but I was beginning to understand that nobody messed with Vincent, no matter how peeved they were.

Sonny had put up a hell of a fight, judging by the smorgasbord of broken bones, gashes, and bruises Azrael was sporting after their encounter. But, as far as I knew, they both had come out of it pretty evenly, so I wasn't overly perturbed.

"She did have sex with Sonny, though," Poppy added, stopping Azrael dead in his tracks. He immediately turned to face me.

"Ohmygod, Poppy!" I shrieked. "What the hell did I tell you?"

"Um, that last night's sex-fest was the best—"

"*Not that part*!"

"Oh, right. You said that I was not to breathe a word about what happened to anyone ever, and in particular, I was never to tell Azrael."

"And what did you just do?" I screeched.

"I told Azrael." She beamed. "Look, just because you tell me to do something, doesn't mean I have to do it. You're not the boss of me."

"I am too the boss of you! When I tell you to do something—"

"I'm sorry, but did I hear right?" Azrael interrupted, still standing with the fridge door open, a tub of yogurt in one hand, and a block of cheddar cheese in the other (what the hell kind of sandwich was he even making?). "You had sex with *Sonny*?"

"She sure did," Poppy chirped, eager to share all the sordid details of my triste. "Like I was saying, she said it was the best—"

"Poppy!" I yelled. "Stop talking. This is not your story to tell."

"But if I don't tell it, I know you won't, and then Azrael would never know—"

"That's the point, you nincompoop!"

"Ah, ah, ah," she sing-songed. "I thought we were trying to be nicer to me."

"That's before you gave up all my sex secrets to the Grim Reaper."

Azrael was suspiciously quiet, as he clutched his snacks. His eyes were wide and his mouth slightly open, and he had the most peculiar expression on his face, like he wanted to tell me something, but also wanted to hear the details of the sexy time.

"And what are you looking at?" I snapped. "You got something to say about this?"

Azrael's face split into one of the widest grins he'd ever graced me with. "Oh man, do I have something to say. But first, I have questions."

"Fire away," Poppy said. "I know all the deets."

"Will you shut up, please?" I said. "There will be no questions. There will be no blow-by-blow account of anything. I'm not here to titillate you. In fact, go away. This is none of your business."

"But I don't want to go away," she moaned. "I want to stay and hear this."

"No. You're going to do as you're told and leave, and I will have a civilized conversation with Azrael, which does not involve *you* telling him all *my* secrets!"

"That's not fair," Poppy said, stamping her foot. She could be so juvenile sometimes. "You said you wouldn't—"

"Get out," I said, pointing to the door, which was kind of ridiculous because it's not like she ever used the damn thing to make her entrances or exits. "Get out and don't come back until I say you can."

You're such a b-i-t-c-h," she said, spelling out the word. "You never let me have any fun."

"Out!"

"Fine, but I'm not happy about it."

"My heart bleeds."

"We're going to have words, later."

"If you say so," I said, waggling my fingers at Poppy. "But for now, bye-bye."

Poppy poked her tongue out at me as she disappeared.

"Finally," I said, turning back to Azrael. "I thought she'd never leave."

He didn't respond, only grinned at me like some deranged Cheshire cat.

"Why the hell are you looking at me like that?" I asked.

"Because, boy oh boy, do I need to school you in the ways of the lycans," he said. "But I think, nay I *know*, you're going to hate what I have to say."

I frowned at him. "Then what's with the toothy grin? You're not having a stroke, are you?"

Azrael shook his head. "No, but after I'm done telling you what I have to tell you, *you* just might."

EIGHT

"WHAT DO YOU MEAN werewolves mate for life?" I said. (Some might say that I was screeching at that moment. I chose to reserve judgement.)

"Just what I said," Azrael replied. "When werewolves reach sexual maturity, they choose a mate—a life mate. They do a little of the horizontal mambo at the full moon, and hey, presto! That's it for them. It's a 'til death do us part' kind of situation."

"It sounds ridiculous if you ask me," I said, ringing my hands.

"Actually, life mates are more common than you might realize."

"Bullshit," I scoffed. "Half the people I know are either divorced or are the products of broken homes. Not to mention all the serial monogamists with deep-seated abandonment issues and crippling fear of intimacy I've dated—"

"Um, you're forgetting something important," Azrael said. "Werewolves might look human, but they aren't. They're animals, well-groomed, highly evolved, *monogamous* animals."

I scowled at him. "Oh, please. What the hell kind of animal mates for life?"

"Well, penguins, puffins, and field mice, for starters. Let's see, beavers, gibbons, seahorses, and let's not forget the good old *canis lupus*—or gray wolf to you." Azrael was still grinning like a damn fool, while I was hyperventilating like a hippo running a marathon.

"But I'm not a werewolf," I whined.

"Part of you is," he said. "The most important part, as it turns out." He tapped his chest and winked at me.

I was getting so tired of hearing that.

"Well, I think that's absurd. Mating for life. It's ridiculous," I insisted. "Surely, this rule doesn't apply to me. I'm only an organ recipient, not a pure blood."

Azrael patted me on the hand. "Sweetie, you can try to rationalize or find loopholes all you want, but it's not going to change the fact that you and Sonny are now mated. From a werewolf perspective, that is."

The mere thought of having to spend my entire life with Sonny was terrifying, and if I was being honest, a little exhilarating, too. Which I'm sure was being driven by my wayward libido, but I wasn't about to let Azrael know that.

"But I didn't know the rules! No one ever mentioned any bloody rules!"

"Ignorance of the law is no excuse," he said, with a smirk. "That's basic year eight legal studies."

"I never took legal studies."

"Yes, you did. Remember, Mr. Claughton? You sat in the back row. You got a B."

"Is there anything you don't remember about my life, you weird creeper?" I said, but Azrael just kept smiling at me. "Okay, fine. You win. I got a B. I just don't understand how this happened." I put my head between my knees and fisted my hair. "I just don't believe it."

But I was lying. I did *believe* it. Not only did I believe it, but I *knew* it. And I knew it because I could *feel* it.

I remembered how it felt, being with Sonny, feeling exposed and vulnerable, yet somehow strong and empowered. The feeling of being totally free; of being totally me. The memory of moving with him in perfect synchronicity, of tasting him, touching him, and being tasted and touched in return. Of bending and writhing with every thrust, every kiss, falling deeper with every lusty murmur.

I knew there was something different going on at the time. It felt significant. It somehow felt…right. But I'd chosen to dismiss it all as post-coital fuzzies, as the crazed ramblings of a sex-addled brain. I'd been on a veeeerrrry long, and unwanted, sex hiatus. It stood to reason my synapses were misfiring.

But then I remembered all the strange thoughts that had flooded my mind, during and afterward; the words that kept echoing over and over in my brain:

Just for me.

Only me.

Mine.

Forever.

And ever.

"But it's not fair. I'm not a real werewolf," I moaned, but there was very little conviction behind my protest. "That has to make a difference?"

Azrael shrugged. "I don't know, you tell me. Does it? Or does the fact your werewolf heart is now the core of your very being change things?"

I threw my head back and mock cried, then sat upright. "Wait, did he know about this?"

"Who?"

"What do you mean who? Sonny, who else?"

"Oh, well yes. Absolutely. He definitely knew."

WHAAAAT?

"Why would he, you know, participate in the activity if he knew what it meant?"

"Well, I can't say for certain."

"You know what, never mind. As far as I'm concerned, it never happened, and I'm just going to ignore it. They can't make me stick to their stupid life mate rule, anyway. It's simply not enforceable. I'm not even a real werewolf and I just won't do it." I slapped my hands together and rubbed my palms. "Case closed."

"You seem to have misunderstood, Clarissa," Azrael said. "This life mate thing, it's not a regulation the lycans or the Patrons just made up. They don't police it."

"Even better," I replied.

Azrael sighed. "No. Not better. This isn't lycan law. It's lycan nature. Instinct. Nobody tricked you into mating with Sonny. You did it all of your own free will. Your heart *chose* him."

"What? That's ridiculous."

"And yet."

"Why would it do that? Why would you do that?" I said, talking to my chest.

"Love?"

I spluttered. "Love? That's just…craziness. It's… It's crazy."

Azrael shrugged. "Okay. If you say so, but if it's not love, I couldn't even begin to imagine why you chose Sonny. You're the only one who knows the answer to that."

Ah, poop.

NINE

IT'S NOT OFTEN I HAVE THE CHANCE TO STEAL A $200,000 MUSCLE CAR and take it for a joyride, but after my conversation with Azrael, *borrowing* his beloved Monaro and fanging it down the Western Highway seemed like a perfectly legitimate way to blow off steam.

What I hadn't counted on, however, was being pulled over by an unmarked Highway Patrol car on a poorly lit section of the road, somewhere between Blackwood and Trentham. Although, in hindsight, I probably should have expected it because traveling at 130km/h in an 80 zone was bound to attract some attention.

Azrael was going to kill me. Kill me for stealing his car, kill me for speeding, and definitely kill me for getting caught.

I was a dead woman walking.

I briefly toyed with the idea of waiting until the patrol officer got within a couple of feet of the Monaro and just flooring it, *Dukes of Hazard*-style. A quick, easy escape.

But I knew that'd be pointless because eventually they'd just catch up with me and I'd get pinged for speeding *and* resisting arrest, or something stupid like that. The police were, after all, cruising around in a brand-new BMW M5 that could suck the doors clean off the fifty-year-old *Holden* I was driving, even with a fully loaded 454 rumbling in the engine bay. I mean, the Monaro was a thing of beauty, don't get me wrong, but it couldn't compete with something that went from zero to 100 in under four seconds.

I glanced at the clock on the dashboard: 12:25. Didn't the police have better things to do at that time of the night? Shouldn't they be breaking up a cock-fighting ring, or raiding a uni house party and confiscating a bunch of Coke can bongs?

Clearly not, because there they were, killing my buzz, and ruining my already ruined night.

I shifted the transmission into neutral and tapped the accelerator, gunning the massive V8 before turning it off and pulling the keys from the ignition. As I reached across the console and pulled my driver's license from my purse, I ran scenarios in my head, trying to come up with something—*anything*—that could pass as a reasonable excuse for my late-night, high-speed jaunt. It's not like I could tell the truth, was it?

"Good evening, Officer. Yes, I understand I was doing a touch over the speed limit, but I needed to blow off a little steam because I just found out I've inadvertently betrothed myself— FOR LIFE—to a man with impeccable abs and questionable morals, who I'm not even sure I like, because apparently I'm bound by werewolf laws through no fault of my own, and no one bothered to tell me about their stupid life mate rules. Can I go now?'

Who the hell was going to believe that cockamamie story? I'd be locked up quicker than you could say *buuuuuullshhhit.*

With red and blue lights flashing in the rear vision mirror, and a patrol officer approaching the car, I wound down the window and plastered on the most innocent, "what seems to be the problem officer?" expression I could muster without looking deranged.

I was totally praying the patrol officer was a guy, more specifically, a guy who liked girls. Or a girl who liked girls. *Anyone* who liked girls really, because I wasn't above flirting (or crying) my way out of this situation, no matter who the flirtee was.

"Where's the fire, mate?" the patrol officer asked as he leaned into the open driver's side window.

I was momentarily blinded by the fifty gajillion-watt flashlight he shone in my face, and wondered if I might need to add night vision and light sensitivity to the ever-growing list of weird werewolf shit I'd have to learn to live with.

Urgh.

FML.

"Do you have any idea how fast you were going?"

I raised my hand, shading my eyes from the flashlight, and my heart sank because right there in front of me was my favorite police officer in the world, Senior Constable Gregory Allan.

There were 16,000 members of the Victorian police force. How—*HOW*—did I manage to get pulled over by the same one, not once but *TWICE*, in three weeks?

I sank down into the driver's seat as far as I could and did my best to conceal my face. Part of me was clinging to the faint hope he wouldn't remember me. I mean, he was a police officer, after all. Surely, he dealt with weirder people and stranger cases than mine, right? Having said that, how often did he come across an insane person who'd just escaped from a body bag careening out the back of a hearse?

Of course, the moment we locked eyes, SC Allan lowered his torch and smiled like he was Ahab and I was his personal *Moby Dick*. The one that got away.

My jig was well and truly up.

"Well, hello there, Ms. Hunt," he said, tipping the brim of his hat. "What a surprise."

I sighed and lowered the hand I'd been using to shield my face. "Senior Constable." I nodded. "Nice to see you again," I lied.

"Yes, I'm sure it is. Let me guess, you're running late for an appointment?"

"No."

"You're in a hurry to get to the hospital to see your grandma before she dies?"

"No."

"Desperately in need of a poop?"

Ass.

Sweat.

Everywhere.

I shook my head.

"But you've got a really good excuse for speeding tonight, am I right?" SC Allan asked.

"Yes." I nodded. "I do."

"This ought to be good," he said, planting his hands on his hips. "Care to share it with me?"

I sighed and shook my head. "No."

"I thought as much. Okay, then, let's get this party started." He stuck out his hand. "Can I have your license, please? Assuming you have it on you this time?"

"Yes, I do," I said, handing over the plastic card.

SC Allan took it from me and examined it. "Nice photo."

"Thank you for noticing. I actually spent two hours with Miss Lisa getting my roots touched up and forty-five minutes having my makeup professionally done before getting that taken," I said, pointing at the photo.

"Why?" He couldn't look more bored if he nodded off.

"It's a ten-year license. I wanted to make sure I looked as good as possible if I was going to be forced to whip that sucker out every time I tried to get into a club or order porn—er, booze. I mean booze. Not porn." I so meant porn. "For a decade."

"Fascinating."

"My cousin Drew always teases me about how much time it takes me to look natural. Hehe."

SC Allan scribbled something in his notebook. "Thanks for the backstory. You'll have to tell me that again sometime."

Asshat.

"Just sit tight while I go run your details," he said without even looking up. "You know the routine."

I did indeed, so I nodded as he walked back to his car to consult with his little on-board computer thingy. I said a little prayer that the hospital, or the coroner, or whoever, had updated my information on their database, because the last thing I wanted was another, *but the system says you're dead* conversation. I just didn't have the energy.

After what felt like an eternity, I spotted SC Allan approaching the Monaro in the rear vision mirror and held my breath.

"Okay, so, the good news is you're not dead," SC Allan said, handing back my license.

"No shit," I mumbled.

He glanced at me and raised a brow, so I smiled back at him. "Any alcohol tonight?"

I shook my head. "I wish."

He slipped a handheld breathalyzer from his utility belt and clicked a fresh plastic tube to the top. "I'll just get you to do a quick breath test. One long breath into the mouthpiece until I tell you to stop."

I did as I was told. This was at least one test I knew I could pass. I hadn't had a drink in days.

The breathalyzer made a high-pitched beep after about fifteen seconds, so SC Allan pulled it from my lips, and peered at the digital display.

"All good." He nodded, removing the used mouthpiece, and returning the device to its holster.

"Now, please step out of the vehicle."

"What? Why?" I asked, tightening my grip on the steering wheel. "I'm not drunk."

"Because I asked you to," came his curt reply.

Was it too late to do a runner?

I let out a long breath and flung the door open, nearly cleaning up SC Allan in the process. "Sorry," I mumbled. "Don't seem to know my own strength." I slammed the door and sagged against the rear-quarter panel.

He smiled tightly. "Can you tell me whose car is this?"

"Yes," I said.

"And that would be…?" SC Allan rolled his hands in front of him, the universal gesture for, *get on with the damn story, woman.*

"Um, it's my friend's car," I croaked, a knot of nervous tension lodging in the base of my throat.

"And what's your friend's name?"

"Azrael," I replied.

"Azrael what?"

I had no idea what Azrael's last name was. I didn't even know if he *had* a last name.

FML x 2.

"Um, actually I don't know," I said, squirming a little. My police-induced ass sweat was trickling its way down into my butt. "We haven't known each other that long."

FML x 3.

Mental note: find out Azrael's last name.

"And this person, your good friend, whose full name you don't know, is he aware you're currently in possession of his vehicle?"

"Sure," I squeaked, hoping Azrael hadn't reported it stolen or anything.

SC Allan scratched his head and scribbled something else in his notepad.

What in the hell was he writing?

"Well, looks like you're going to have to tell Mr. Azrael his car is being impounded," he said without looking up from his notebook,

"*What*?"

"For a month."

"I said, *whaaaat*?"

SC Allan looked up. "This car," he shouted, slowly pointing to the Monaro as if I was hard of hearing. *Dipshit*. "Is being impounded…" Still speaking lower than a snail wading through molasses. "For *twentyyyyy-eiiiight* days."

God, I hated him. He was a smartass, just like Sonny only not—*wait*. Did he say twenty-eight days?

"*Twenty-eight days*?"

He nodded.

"*Whyyyy*?" I whined.

"Because according to my radar, you were travelling 130km/h in an 80 zone."

"That can't be right," I said, frowning. "Are you sure?"

"Am I sure?" He laughed. "Yeah, one hundred percent. You can look at the reading yourself if you want," he offered, pointing to his car.

"No, it's fine," I replied. I knew exactly how fast I'd been going. I was only trying to buy myself some time.

"I'll also be issuing you with a ticket, it comes with a fine of $925."

Crap, crappity, crap, crap.

"Your license will also be suspended for twelve months, and it'll cost about $1,000 to get the car out of impound."

To say I was shocked and stunned would be an understatement of epic proportions. I mean, how was I going to get to Ruby's cafe every morning for my double-shot caramel, almond milk Frappuccino? Or the gym, for that matter? (Not that I'd set foot in a gym since, well, ever.) I was going to have to sign up to Uber One, wasn't I?

"Is the license suspension effective immediately?" I asked, my voice going up three octaves on *immediately*.

He shook his head. "No. You've got a month. Plenty of time to sort out your affairs, let your boss know, cancel your appointments, download a bus schedule." SC Allan chuckled.

Bastard.

"And when will the car be impounded?"

SC Allan pointed at his partner, who was in the passenger seat of the Beamer, talking on his phone. "He's calling the towey now. Should be here in about an hour."

"An hour? Are you *kidding me*?"

"Do I look like I'm kidding?"

"No, you kind of look like you've got a broom stuck up your ass," I grumbled.

"Pardon?" he asked, brows raised.

"Nothing. You were saying?"

"An hour is plenty of time to get all your stuff out of the vehicle."

"And what am I supposed to do after that?" I threw my hands in the air. "I'm in the middle of nowhere. It's pitch dark. You're at least going to give me a ride home, right?"

SC Allan smirked. "Yeah, right."

I stared at him and he straightened.

"Oh, you're serious." He corrected himself, "Sorry. Yeah, nah."

"So, what, you're just going to leave me here to fend for myself? Are you *crazy*?"

He smiled tightly.

"Like I said." He tapped his wristwatch. "You've got about an hour to call someone to come get you. A friend? Fiancé? Mr. Azrael, maybe?"

"He's hardly going to pick me up if you're impounding his car, is he?" I sniped.

"Daddy, then? Or maybe the muscle-bound goons who rescued you from the police station?"

Oh, and I could just imagine how that conversation would go. *Hey, Vincent, Sonny, could you come get me from the Bacchus Marsh lock up? I've been arrested again.*

No, thank you.

"Don't we think it's a bit late to be phoning someone for a ride?" I asked.

SC Allan shrugged. "You'll have to work something out. It's getting cold out." He finally closed his notebook and slipped it into the side pocket of his tactical vest. "You don't want to catch something, do you?"

And that's how I found myself on the side of a highway at 1:30 in the morning, watching Azrael's prized Monaro get hoisted onto a flatbed, and waiting for Manjeet, my Uber driver, to pick me up.

He was twelve minutes away, according to my app.

Senior Constable Allan and his off-sider, Constable Brown, were still hanging around, even though they'd finished their paperwork. Despite all his smarmy blustering, I think SC Allan might actually have taken a shine to me and maybe wasn't entirely comfortable leaving me alone and vulnerable on the side of a highway.

If only he knew the half of it.

"So," SC Allan said as he joined me on the verge. "How's Keith?"

"Who?" I asked, frowning at him in the dim moonlight.

"You know, *Keith*, your boyfriend. The pervert funeral director."

I coughed, then spluttered.

"Oh, *that* Keith," I replied. "Um, we broke up."

"That's a shame. You seemed like such a lovely couple." he said.

My ass was sweating like I was on the Nullarbor, in the middle of summer, wearing a woolen suit lined in tin foil.

"Not that old Keithy realized just how serious your relationship was."

I ran my hands down my face. This guy was *killing* me. "Well, I don't think we'd ever said we were exclusive."

"Must have been hard for him, losing his job, breaking up with you, his wife leaving him."

"His wife left him, *and* he lost his job?"

"Sure, but he should be able to get another one eventually," he continued. "A job that is. Not a wife. Just as soon as he completes his sex offender rehabilitation program and registers as a necrophiliac."

Wait. "*What?*"

"Well, because of the statement you gave us, we had to investigate him further; do a deep-dive into his professional and private life. Because, let's face it, if he needed you to play dead just so the two of you could, you know." He made a gesture with his hands that suggested intercourse. "He was bound to be interfering with the real bodies, right? And that's a *b-i-i-i-g* no-no in his industry."

Ass sweat was running down the back of my legs and past my knees. Oh, God.

"I mean, we couldn't find any *actual* evidence that proved he was a necrophiliac. He'd done a brilliant job covering his tracks. I'm talking crystal clean. If it wasn't for you and your statement, we would have thought he was one hundred percent innocent."

Holllyyyyyyy. Shiiiittttt!

"Don't worry, though. We tucked him away in remand for a couple of nights and made sure his cell mates knew all about his sexual preferences." SC Allan winked. "I'm sure they treated him with the same dignity and respect he showed his victims."

This could not be happening.

It had to be some kind of terrible dream.

What kind of horrible, horrible person was I?

"What's the matter?" SC Allan asked, frowning. "You look a little pale."

Pale? That wasn't the half of it. I couldn't speak. I could barely breathe, and I'm pretty sure my heart had completely seized up...and I actually knew what that felt like.

How could I have been so stupid? So selfish? I hadn't even thought about the impact my lies could have had on poor Keith. I'd only thought about myself and basically ruined his life. He'd been labeled a pervert, lost his job, his family, and I couldn't even begin to imagine what he'd gone through at the Remand Center.

I felt sick, like I was going to puke right there on SC Allan's shiny black boots.

"You alright?" I heard him ask, but he sounded like he was a million miles away.

I was going to hell. I was going to burn in eternal damnation for my deception, and selfishness, and general horribleness.

And it would totally be the right call.

I decided there and then that all this was going to stop, immediately.

No more lies.

No more blaming others or concocting wild stories just to keep myself out of trouble. I was going to come clean, take full responsibility for all my actions. I was going to tell the truth—

"Take a breath, Clarissa," SC Allan said with a smirk. "Nothing happened to Keith."

—clean up my act and...wait. "*What*?" My mouth dropped open and my eyes practically bugged out of my head. "What did you say?"

"Like I was ever going to believe a single word of that cock-

and-bull story you spun me," he said, shaking his head. "How dumb do you think I am?"

"I don't think you're dumb, but I'm beginning to get the feeling you're a little cruel," I replied.

Of all the police officers in Victoria, I had to get the one with the macabre sense of whimsy and evil sense of humor.

The one who clearly hated me.

And thought I was a liar.

Which, in his defense, was an accurate assessment of my character these days.

"I don't know who you are, Clarissa, or what you're mixed up in, but I didn't come down in the last shower."

"I never said you did."

"Your friends might have scared my sergeant, but let me tell you, I'm not so easily intimidated."

"Good to know," I said.

Bright headlights approached from the east, distracting us both. The driver indicated left and the vehicle eased off the road, coming to a stop not far behind the BMW.

"Uber's here," Constable Brown called out, and SC Allan offered me a hand up, which I gratefully took. I'd been sitting on cold rocks for an hour, so everything below my waist had gone numb.

"Saved by the Uber," I said, dusting off the seat of my pants. "If you'll excuse me."

As I brushed past SC Allan, he took my arm. Not hard or aggressively in any way, but just enough to stop me in my tracks.

"I'm keeping an eye on you, Clarissa," he said. "24/7/365."

"Excellent," I replied, extricating my arm from his grasp. "I feel safer already."

TEN

I WAS GETTING PRETTY TIRED of waking up in dank, dark places, not knowing where the hell I was or how long I'd been there.

At least I wasn't in a body bag this time, or careening out the back of a moving vehicle, so that was a plus.

I sat up on what turned out to be a slimy, bluestone floor in a dimly lit, cavernous room that reeked of damp earth and rotting garbage.

Scurrying noises in the shadowy corners, and high in the rafters, made my skin crawl and I wondered what beasties might be lurking in the inky darkness.

Goblins?

Imps?

Or worse...*rats*?

The dungeon—there really was no other word to describe it —was miserably bleak and bare, offering little in the way of hope or escape.

Just another day at the office, right?

My head pounded, the pain radiating from the base of my skull right into the backs of my eyes. It was a legit headache, too, not one of the fake *period* migraines I used to get out of going to dinner with that snooze-worthy IT guy I met on PoF. I'd only done that once.

Okay, maybe twice.

Three times, but that's it.

This headache was definitely real, and it was a monster.

I gingerly ran my hand over the back of my head and found the egg-sized lump that was causing all the pain. Someone had clobbered me hard.

The hair around the lump was sticky and matted. It could have been blood, or it could have been the disgusting goo I'd been lying in. Either way, a visit to Miss Lisa was definitely in order, because let's face it, she and her magical hands were the only things I knew of that could possibly sort out the icky mess back there.

Although, I should probably get checked out by a doctor first, you know, before I booked the appointment to fix my blowout because…priorities.

I stared at the dreary surroundings and tried to figure out how the hell I'd managed to get myself into what was likely another life-or-death situation.

The last thing I remembered prior to waking up in the goop was watching Azrael's car being towed, having a very unpleasant conversation about necrophilia with SC Allan, and then wondering why my Uber driver had fangs.

Of course, Uber drivers don't have fangs, not the human ones, anyway. This guy, and the three sidekicks he had tucked away in the back of his Prius, was neither an Uber driver, nor a human.

I remember scrambling into the Highway Patrol car after SC Allan emptied not one but two full clips—that's fifteen rounds *each*—from his Smith and Wesson, straight into the chest of the vamp who jumped us. Not that it had done any good. It's not like forty-caliber hollow points have any effect on vampires. No sooner had I made it into the patrol car, I got yanked straight back out again, and SC Allan was nowhere to be seen. It was like he disappeared into thin air.

At the time, I hoped he'd escaped, but with the benefit of hindsight, I wasn't convinced he had.

I remembered there being a scuffle, there may have been biting (me, not the vampires), and I vaguely recalled ripping the head off at least one of the bloodsuckers before somebody cracked me on the noggin. After that, it was lights out.

I rubbed my eyes and groaned. Why did all this shit keep happening to me? I used to lead such a normal, happy life—heart disease and the loss of my sister notwithstanding. There were no kidnappings, no murders, no dying and waking up in body bags or falling out of hearses. Just work, dinners with friends, running the dating gauntlet, ice hockey games in the winter, summers at the holiday house in Point Lonsdale. It was a nice, comfortable life.

I liked that life.

I missed that life.

This new life felt like I was living in an episode of the Twilight Zone—reality edition.

I tried not to think about the absolute shit fit Vincent was going to have once he found out about this little misadventure. There was a very good chance it might just push him completely over the edge, and if I did eventually get out of this predicament alive, he'd just kill me anyway. Not that I blamed him. I really was prone to getting myself into impossible situations.

I patted myself down, just to make sure all my other bits were intact. I didn't seem to have any additional bumps, lumps, cuts, or scrapes. No stab wounds, bullet holes, or vampire bites.

Small mercies.

As I frisked myself, I was equal parts relieved, and

astounded, to discover whoever kidnapped me had been stupid enough to leave my mobile phone in the back pocket of my jeans.

Gotta love a dumb bloodsucker, right?

I immediately pulled it out and prayed it still had a charge. There was no telling how long I'd been unconscious. Could have been an hour, could have been a week. When I tapped the screen and the phone lit up, I almost wept, first with joy—seventy-eight percent charge…yay!—and then with horror when I noticed the giant crack splitting it down the middle.

The phone cast an eerie bluish light, revealing more of my gloomy surroundings. As predicted, I was definitely in a dungeon, complete with chunky rafters, high, iron-barred windows, and an enormous wooden door that reminded me of the ones that separate the subterranean levels of the cathedral. Heavy shackles hung around the room and unlit wooden torches lined the walls without windows.

Just how long had I been unconscious? Had I been shipped off to England or France or something? Because this place oozed with the kind of ghoulish charm you'd only expect to see in Europe. It was medieval architecture at its finest, and I was pretty sure we didn't have any of that in Melbourne. Unless you counted Kryal Castle, but this place didn't exactly feel like a theme park offering supervised kid's archery adventures on Tuesdays and jousting on the third Sunday of every month.

This place felt pretty damn authentic.

An unexpected rattling in the darkened corner to my left startled me so much, I actually shrieked…and maybe peed myself a little. Not my finest moment. Definitely one to be filed away under 'Never to be Mentioned Again', a list that was growing longer and much faster than I would have liked.

I tapped the torch button on the phone and shone it into the darkness, my heart thumping and palms sweating in anticipation.

It didn't take long to find the pathetic figure of a disheveled man cowering in the corner. He was blood-smeared and bruised, slick with sweat, grime and, most concerning, he wasn't moving all that much.

This someone was severely injured.

I shuffled over to him, giving him a gentle shake, and rousing him. Bloodshot eyes peered up at me. He seemed disoriented, confused, bound by shiny silver chains that wrapped around most of his torso.

"Are you okay?" I asked.

Of course he wasn't okay. He looked like he'd been through a meat grinder.

"Are you injured?"

I'd seen corpses with better coloring. I'd *been* a corpse with better coloring.

"Yes," came his feeble reply.

"Where?"

"Please, you must remove the chains. They are killing me."

I nodded and wrapped my hands around the shiny links, startled by the way they tingled and sizzled in my hands. It was a familiar sensation; one I'd never forget. The last time I'd felt it, I had a ten-inch silver dagger shoved into my chest.

I continued to struggle with the chains, but not even my newfound werewolf super-strength could budge them.

"They're silver," the old man said. "Werewolf kryptonite."

"Oh, I know," I said, remembering the searing pain the dagger had caused.

"Do you know where we are?" I asked, suddenly feeling completely drained. I let the silver chains slip from my hands.

"Vampire nest," he wheezed

"How did you get here?"

"I don't know."

"How did I get here?"

He stared at me.

"Right. Well, do you know how *long* you've been here?"

"Longer than you."

"Do you know how long *I've* been here?"

"Not as long as me."

Oh, this conversation was going well, wasn't it? Not at all difficult or at all frustrating.

"You are Clarissa, no?" he asked, squinting at me.

"No," I replied. "Wait, no. I mean, yes. I'm Clarissa. Do I know you?"

"In a way."

This gentleman was about as forthcoming with the details as Vincent, which was not an endearing quality.

"It is I, Silvio."

Silvio?

Lightbulb! Ring-a-ding-ding.

"The werewolf alpha?" I gaped.

"At your service." He nodded.

I peered at him. This couldn't possibly be the Silvio I'd met. This guy was old and frail and gross; not at all the handsome, enigmatic, and cultured man who commanded the lycans in all four quadrants.

Maybe I had been unconscious longer than I thought because I'd only seen this guy like a week ago, and he looked a million years older than he had then.

"And you," he continued. "You are Vincent's experiment, no? Sorry. I mean, hybrid?"

"Well, at least you didn't call me an abomination," I said. "That's a nice change."

"I never called you that."

"No. Your daughter did."

"She has a mind of her own," he said with a small shake of his head.

"She's a bitch," I said. "Sorry."

"No need to apologize. It's not your fault." Silvio snorted.

"I'm surprised you are here. I thought you were, how you say...*eliminata*."

I sat back on my haunches. "Eliminated?"

Silvio tried to straighten himself, but almost immediately slumped backward against the cold, damp wall. Our eyes met and he nodded. "The Peacekeeper. The very big one."

"Sonny?"

"Si. He didn't do such a good job, killing you, did he?" There was a tone to his voice, a hint of amusement, maybe? "Yet somehow, I don't believe he's incompetent."

"No, he's not." I shrugged. "I'll tell you what he is, though. He's a chauvinistic, macho schmuck who, okay, might be superficially attractive—I mean the guy has abs for days—and don't get me started on his, err... Never mind."

"Schmuck?"

"Exactly." I repositioned myself and took hold of the chains again, determined to free Silvio before he deteriorated further.

"Of course, if you take all that away, the hotness and the ah-maz-ing body, what's left? Nothing, that's what." I continued to struggle with the chains, but they refused to budge. "Okay, so maybe he's strong and brave, and sure, he can be sweet, when he's not *killing* you. And fine, he might just be the best sex a girl ever had, but let's not forget he's also a thug, and quite frankly, someday..." I was yanking on the damn chains so hard, I nearly tore my rotator cuff. It was futile.

I dropped them again, leaning back again and throwing my hands in the air. "I don't understand why I can't break these stupid things. Are they cursed or something?"

Silvio was staring at me with that puzzled expression I was growing accustomed to seeing, the one when people were having trouble deciphering my nonstop yammering.

I really had to use my internal filter more often.

Or at all.

"I told you, they're silver. Werewolves are powerless against silver."

"Which would be a problem if I was a werewolf." I stood and planted my hands on my hips and scanned the room.

"There is more werewolf in you than you think," Silvio wheezed. "Your inability to break the chains is confirmation."

"This is no good," I said, getting frustrated. "We have to find a way out, because it doesn't take a genius to see this isn't the Marriott and we won't be enjoying complimentary cocktails or gorging on the all-you-can-eat seafood buffet anytime soon."

"You're a strange woman," Silvio said. "Strange and disagreeable. But, intriguing."

"Was that meant to be a compliment?"

"What do you think?"

I was starting to feel like Old Mate might actually deserve to be chained up in the dungeon after all, and briefly contemplated leaving him behind after I worked out how to make my escape. But a strange tug in my heart told me that wouldn't be the right thing to do. Turning my back on this helpless man would be, well, unforgivable.

"First, you need to get me out of these," he said, rattling the chains.

"I've been trying, remember?"

"No, you don't understand. You *must* free me, not just for my sake, but for yours. When the *sanguisugi* return, they will be thirsting for blood. You will need my help to defend yourself."

"Why, because I'm a woman? Because I couldn't possibly be strong enough or skilled enough to protect us both? You'd be surprised at how much damage I can do on my own," I said.

"I don't think I'd be surprised at all. Your reputation precedes you. But no, I do not think you need my help because you're a woman. I think you need my help because you are still somewhat human."

"Somewhat? I thought you just said I was a werewolf?" I said, narrowing my eyes.

"You are something in between," he replied, a strange softness in his eyes, the hint of a smile on his lips. "And that makes you vulnerable."

I couldn't argue with that.

With each word he spoke, I could tell the silver chains were weakening him. If I didn't free Silvio quickly, and get us the hell out of the stinky dungeon, it was going to be curtains for both of us.

"What do they want with us, anyway?" I asked as Silvio continued to struggle. He was in bad shape and it was just a matter of time before he'd succumb to their destructive power.

He sighed. "Someone in my position expects assassination attempts and kidsnappings."

"It's kidnapping," I said.

"What did I say?"

"Kidsnappings."

Silvio shrugged. "I don't hear the difference."

"It's… You know what? Never mind. Continue."

"Where was I?"

"Kidsnappings."

"*Si*. I expect these things, but not you. You must have a Blood Bounty on your head." Silvio managed to get to his knees but didn't have the strength to stand up under his own steam. Still, it was the most I'd seen him move since I found him. "This says you must be very special."

"Does it?"

"*Certo*. The *sanguisugi*, they do not declare Blood Bounties weelly-neelly."

Weelly-neelly? Did he mean, willy-nilly? Ohmygod, he was so cute! I just wanted to squish-hug him, which I refrained from doing, because that wouldn't have been at all weird or awkward.

Plus, in his feeble state, I'd probably crush him to death and then I'd really be in big trouble with the lycans.

"Usually, they just rip out the throat and bleed you dry."

"Oh, come on," I said, screwing up my face. "Why are all the paranormal ways of dying always so gross? Seriously."

"Because human ways are so much better?"

Touché.

"Why didn't they just kill me? Why go to the trouble of the Blood Bounty?"

"Is because you are under Vincent's protection, *no*?"

"No?"

"*Si*. Is a brave creature who challenges Vincent and the Patrons."

"Or stupid," I added. "Or even greedy?"

Silvio nodded.

"Hence the Bounty," I said.

"*Esattamente*."

I didn't know what was more confusing, Silvio's convoluted Yoda speak, or the fact that I understood it.

"So, do you have any idea why the vampires want me dead? Surely I'm not that impressive."

"I didn't think so."

Ouch! #selfesteemstrike

"But obviously you are. The *sanguisugi*, they are afraid of you. They see you as a liability." He shook his head. "They are *ignoranti*."

"So, what's your excuse?" I asked, feeling along the basalt and red brick wall for the fastening that secured the chains.

Silvio frowned. "I don't understand. I don't see you as a risk. I see you as an opportunity."

"Yet, you want me dead, too."

As suspected, while the chains wrapped around Silvio were silver, the large ring that secured them to the wall was not. It was iron. If I could dislodge the ring, I was pretty sure I'd be able to at least loosen the chains enough for Silvio to free himself and then we could make our escape. That was the plan, anyway.

"I don't want you dead," Silvio said and for some reason, I was inclined to believe him.

"But Donatella does," I said.

"*Si, si*...my daughter, she has the opinions. She is my eldest. It is to be expected."

I looked at Silvio. "I thought Dante was your eldest."

His eyes spoke volumes. All the emotions were there: pain, sadness, turmoil, regret. "Dante is my eldest *son*. Donatella is my eldest *child*."

"So, why isn't *she* your heir?" I asked. "It's because she's a woman, isn't it? Because that's bullshit. This is the 21st century, you know. That kind of antiquated, sexist thinking just doesn't fly anymore."

Silvio raised his brows and smiled. "Now you sound like her."

I wiped my slime-covered hands on the legs of my jeans which, PS: were going straight into the incinerator (no amount of Napisan was ever going to get rid of this amount of yuck) and grabbed the iron ring. Leaning back as far as I could without falling, I pulled. And pulled. And pulled. And pulled.

Nothing.

It didn't budge. It didn't even wiggle. Not even a millimeter.

Sonofabitch.

Readjusting my position, I widened my stance, and planted my right foot on the wall halfway between the ring and the floor. I braced myself, leaned back farther, and pulled again. Harder this time, and to my relief, I felt it loosen a smidge.

Aha! Progress.

"Clarissa," Silvio said.

"Not now," I replied. "I've almost got it."

I stretched my neck from side to side and shook out both shoulders, which had tightened up after my silver chain tug-o-war (God, I was out of shape). I did the same with my arms and legs. I wanted to be lithe and limber for this next attempt.

"Clarissa," Silvio repeated.

"Don't worry," I said. "Third time's a charm."

When I leaned back and pulled on the ring again, I threw all my body weight behind it (first time ever I was happy about all the COVID lockdown kilos I'd piled on) and, as hoped, the ring dislodged from the wall with a jerk. I found myself sailing across the dungeon and landing with an undignified plop in a puddle of gooey yuckiness. I held the metal ring in my hand, victorious. "Aha! Got it!"

"Clarissa!" Silvio said, this time with a little more urgency.

"What?" I snapped, glancing up at him.

"Look." He motioned to the high window behind me, the orange-red glow of sunset streaming into the dungeon. "Is getting dark. They will come for us soon," he said.

"Then we really need to get out of here before they do. Can you get yourself free?"

Silvio wriggled against the silver bindings that were still wrapped around his body. "I think so."

"I could try and—"

"Why don't you just call to someone?" he asked. "To help?"

"Sure," I said dryly. "I'll just scream at the top of my lungs and pray some poor, unsuspecting passerby just happens to hear my desperate cries, shall I? Is that the plan?"

"I meant using your phone. Call to someone to come get us."

I glanced at the phone, which I'd put down when I'd started fiddling with the iron fastener, and smacked myself upside the head, but not too hard (I was still nursing that damn migraine). I'd been so fixated on freeing Silvio, I'd completely forgotten the most fundamental of all the escape/rescue strategies going round: use your damn phone and call someone for help.

Urgh. If this were a horror movie, I'd be the chick with the big boobies tripping over my own feet while I was running from the crazed machete-wielding serial killer wearing dungarees and a sports mask.

I scurried back to Silvio and picked up my phone. I held it up to my face and checked my reception.

No bars. Dammit.

I shifted a little to the left.

One bar. Yay!

I shifted a little more to the left.

No bars. Shit. Bugger. Damn.

I moved around the dungeon, holding the phone up over my head like an idiot, trying to get a better signal. 5G, my ass. Screw you and your top-of-the-line communication network guarantee, Telecom, because it wasn't worth the paper it was written on.

I walked around in circles long enough to make myself dizzy, until I finally managed to get two full bars, and practically wept. I scrolled through my contacts, found the name I wanted, Sonny, and tapped his number. The call connected and I waited.

And waited.

And waited.

Pick up, pick up, pick up!

He wasn't picking up.

He wasn't picking up, and my call was going to bloody voicemail. *Hey, you've reached Sonny. You know what to do. Beeeeeeep.*

"Dammit, Sonny. Where are you?" I asked, after the tone. "Three weeks and I can't get rid of you. I turn around and you're always there. Now, when I actually need you, I'm talking to your voicemail?"

"*Clarissa!*" Silvio snapped, as the loosened chains slipped from his body. "*Sbrigati! Get on with it!*"

"Right. Yes. Listen, Sonny, when you get this message, you need to come get us. We've been kidnapped by vampires and I'm pretty sure they're going to finish the job Beverley started—"

My phone started dinging and vibrating in my hand, and

when I glanced at it, I saw Sonny's name flashing on the broken screen.

He was returning my call.

"Oh, thank God," I said, answering immediately. "Sonny! Sonny!" I screeched into the microphone. "Sonny!"

"Clarissa? Can you hear me? Are you okay?"

"No. I'm not okay. I'm sooooo not okay. I've been kidnapped by vampires! You have to come get us and I mean now!"

"Us?"

"Me and Silvio. He's in bad shape. They wrapped him in silver chains."

"Silvio *De Benedetto*?"

"Yes, of course, Silvio De Benedetto. How many other Silvio's do you know?"

"How did you find him?"

"I didn't find him. I told you, I was kidnapped and he was here already."

"Do you know where you are?"

"Yes! We're in the dungeon, in the vampire nest," I said,

"Which vampire nest?" Sonny asked. His voice was dropping in and out, forcing me to keep walking around in circles, phone in the air. I was beginning to feel like the Statue of Liberty.

"What do you mean, *which* vampire nest? There's more than one?"

"There are dozens."

Shitfuckityshitfuck!

"I have no idea. All I know is the sun's going down, I'm pretty sure Silvio's dying."

Silvio gasped.

"Well, he *might* be dying." I shrugged and mouthed, *sorry* at Silvio. I had no idea if he was actually dying or not. I just knew we needed to get out of that horrible place, quick smart.

"...and, unless my ears are deceiving me, someone's headed this way."

I turned my head toward the footfalls my super-wolfie hearing had detected. They were getting louder, and closer. This was so not good.

"Clarissa, the sun, she has gone down," Silvio said. "The *sugasangui*, they come."

"How many?" I asked Silvio. He held up three fingers.

"Sonny! Just hurry up. Do your damn job and find us. I'll do my best to buy some time."

I pressed the side button on the phone, which put it in sleep mode, but didn't disconnect the call. I hoped leaving the line open might provide Sonny with information to help him figure out where we were, assuming we were still in Melbourne. We could have been in fricken Pennsylvania for all I knew.

"I think you mean Transylvania," Silvio corrected.

"Whatever," I grumbled. "Pennsylvania. Transylva—" I spun around. "Wait. Did you just read my mind?"

Silvio nodded. "It seems I did."

Because my life wasn't weird enough.

Was this a shiny new werewolf superpower thingy for me to enjoy? Because it wasn't going to be annoying at all.

"Well, quit it," I snapped. "Stay out of my head."

"Is not intentional, believe me," he grumbled.

I slipped the phone back into my jeans pocket and turned just as the lock clicked, the knob turned and three vampires, in full game face, appeared in the doorway, snarling like pit bulls.

"Let me handle this," I said, stepping between Silvio and the bloodsuckers.

"*Be careful,*" his voice echoed in my head.

"*Goddamn it.*" I replied, and by replied, I mean I thought the words and hoped Silvio could hear them, too. "*You're freaking me out.*"

"*Is freaking me out, too.*"

"Okay, well, just shoosh and try not to—*whoa.*"

The vampires filled the doorway with their long, lean frames, eyes glowing crimson in the dim light. I immediately recognized one of them. Constable Brown.

"I know you!" I said, pointing at the police officer. "You pulled me over on the freeway! Does Senior Constable Allan know you're a dirty double agent?"

"He does now," Brown cackled. "But we don't need to worry about him anymore."

"Asshole," I sneered at Brown. (Who, PS, reminded me of Corey Feldman. Or was it Corey Haim? One of the two, anyway. I could never remember which was which.) I might not have known SC Allan very long, or very well, or at all, really, but somehow, I felt like, with time, we could have become friends. Or acquaintances. Or at least people who could be cordial when one of us broke the law and the other was arresting them. And now he was probably dead, and I'd never know.

"And you." The tallest vampire, who I'm pretty sure was neither called Manjeet nor an Uber driver, pointed at me. "You killed Marco."

I cocked my head. "Did I? I don't remember doing that. Are you sure it was me?"

"You ripped his head clean off," he added, in disgust.

"That certainly sounds like me," I said, grinning at the fanged freaks. "Nice."

"I wouldn't be too cocky," the tall vamp spat. "The next person who loses their head just might be you."

"Wow, that's original," I taunted. I knew I had to buy lots of time so Sonny could find us and save us from what I'm pretty sure was going to be a bloodbath of epic proportions.

"I'm sorry, but you have me at a disadvantage," I said. "You seem to know me, but I don't know you."

"Who we are is none of your business."

"Oh, but I think it is. If you intend to kill me, the least you can do is tell me your names."

"Don't tell her anything, Michael," the wiry, and clearly dopey vampire on the far right said. (Ten bucks says he's the idiot who left my phone in my back pocket.) "Just rip her throat out and be done with it."

I smiled as Michael turned and glared at his offsider. "Nice one, *Ian*," Michael said.

I snort-laughed.

Ian? The vampire's name was Ian?

I felt three pairs of blood-red eyes fall back on me and regained my composure.

"Sorry," I said, checking myself. "Please continue, Michael, is it?"

"You've got a big mouth," Michael said.

"All the better to eat you with," I said with a smirk.

"Was that meant to be funny?"

"Some people might have thought so."

"Not me."

"Not surprising. You need an actual sense of humor to understand jokes. Say, while we're chatting, care to share what happened to Senior Constable Allan?" I asked, directing my question to Brown.

"We took care of him," he replied.

"So you said, but what exactly does that mean?"

"It means he won't be bothering us any time soon," Brown sneered.

Poop. I knew what that meant.

"Well, Constable Brown," I said, feeling surprisingly bad for SC Allan and his untimely demise. "On his behalf, if you or any of your bloodsucking band of not-so-merry-men care to surrender, now's the time. If not, feel free to step on up for a good, old-fashioned ass kicking."

I casually stepped back into the fighting stance Sensei Brett had shown me in my advanced self-defense class, arms loose and limber, front foot light (for quick kicks, checks, blocks, parries and knees), the back heavy, to help keep me balanced and grounded.

"As much as watching you die would bring me immense pleasure, you might want to hold off on the brawling for a minute," Michael said. "We have a little surprise for you."

Ian and Brown stepped outside, and returned a few moments later, grappling with two people with their hands bound. They were putting up a decent fight. My heart sank. It would be Vincent and Sonny, I was sure of it. Why else would they be taking so long to get here?

Playing out like that scene from *Grease* when the Pink Ladies shoved Sandy (RIP Olivia) through the crowd and right in front of Danny at the pep rally, it wasn't until the prisoners were flung to the ground that I realized they weren't in fact Vincent and Sonny. It was Max and Donatella. Disheveled, disoriented, and severely damaged.

I didn't know who looked worse, Silvio or his progeny.

"Massimiliano?" Silvio wheezed. "Donatella? *Cosa sucede*? What's happening?"

"Papá?" Max replied.

"Papá, you're here. You're alive, " Donatella said, scrambling over to her father.

"*Si*," Silvio replied. "*Si*."

"*Grazie a dio*. Everyone has been searching for you. How did you get here?"

Donatella was patting Silvio down, checking for injuries and wriggling the chains completely from his body.

"We don't know."

"We?" Max said.

"*Si*. We." Silvio pointed at me.

Max pivoted, and I gave him a little finger wave. His jaw went slack, and he looked like he'd seen a ghost.

Boy, did I know how that felt.

"I've got everything under control," I said, trying to reassure them all. Of course, I had nothing under control. I had about as much control as…as something that was out of control. On the upside, though, I'd been right about someone having it in for the De Benedettos.

"*You?*" he said, eyes locking with mine. The smell of confusion wafted off him in waves. Confusion, and something else, something like anger, maybe. "*You're alive?*"

I nodded.

Michael and Ian were now circling me, snarling like hyenas, cracking their knuckles, snapping their fangs, and I knew I didn't have a lot of time to gain the upper hand, if any at all.

Where the bloody hell was Sonny, anyway? I'd literally handed him the names of all three vampires. Surely that was enough? There couldn't possibly be that many bloodsuckers named Michael, Ian, and, er, Constable Brown, round these parts, could there?

ELEVEN

AS IT TURNS OUT, when a vampire dies, it bursts into bright blue, then orange flames before disintegrating into ashes that float, ever so gently, to the floor, kind of like snowflakes—if snowflakes were, in fact, made from the remains of blood-sucking fiends.

Who knew?

Dispensing with the three vamps wasn't all that difficult, far less effort than, say, killing Beverley—relatively speaking.

My Wrench and Yank* decapitation move (*patent pending) took care of Ian and Michael just as easily as it had Beverley, leaving nothing but two neat piles of crimson ash at my feet. I dispensed of Constable Brown the old-fashioned way, tearing one of the unlit torches from the bluestone wall and jamming it straight through his heart.

And just like that, there were three little piles of ash.

Which brings me to my second point, dead vampires are *sooooo* much easier to get rid of than werewolves. No way could I have disposed of Bev's manky carcass on my own. That disgusting job required a whole army of paranormal cleaners and detox specialists. But with the bloodsuckers, all I really needed was a *Hoover*...or a brush and pan...or at the very least, a gust of wind.

Mental note: buy a brush and pan set, just in case.

"*Brava*!" Silvio clapped, after I'd dispensed with the bloodsuckers. He was nudging Max and Donatella, encouraging them to applaud my victory. They didn't, of course. No surprises there. They'd made their feelings about me perfectly clear at the POO meeting. I couldn't see that changing any time soon.

"What a battle!" Silvio continued. "What a warrior! You truly have the heart of a werewolf. *Brava*!"

I straightened, *sloooowly*, and rubbed my lower back. "Yeah, well, my heart might be werewolf but the rest of me is human, and the human parts hurt A LOT right now."

I admired my handiwork, enjoying the sense of relief and, if I was being completely honest, gloating a little, before I turned my attention back to more important things, like orchestrating our escape from the pseudo-medieval hellhole.

"Not that this hasn't been a blast or anything," I said, brushing errant flecks of Ian from my jeans. "But I'd like to get out of here before more vamps come looking for their buddies. Plus, I really need a shower, because killing you paranormals is just, wow, disgusting. So, Max, why don't you help your fath—"

As I turned around to workshop an escape plan with Team De Benedetto, I was horrified to see that Max was already attending to Silvio—only he wasn't freeing him. Nope, he was smirking like a giant...er, smirker (whatever, I was tired), and looping the silver chains that had taken me *forever* to loosen, back around Silvio's frail frame. Max's hands smoldered as he handled the silver, but with the exception of the unpleasant stink of singed knuckle hair, the chains didn't seem to bother him all that much.

What the hell was even going on?

Max brushed his palms together and presented them to me. "A little silver doesn't do too much damage," he said as if he was reading my mind. Wait, was he reading my mind? Because if he was, this was clearly going to take some getting used to. "Prolonged exposure on the other hand." He glanced at his father. "And our organs start to cook before they completely shut down. Left long enough, the silver causes a slow and painful death. You'll see it for yourself shortly."

Donatella sat silently on the putrid cobblestone floor, her gaze fixed. Was she paralyzed with fear? Was she in shock? Was she injured? I couldn't tell. But what I did know was she wasn't happy. In fact, she was livid. I could smell the white-hot rage radiating from her.

"Max," she said in a calm tone that defied her anger. "Please, explain yourself."

"I'm afraid we've run into a little problem," Max said, giving his father's chains one final yank. He was looking far less disheveled than he had when he was first thrown into the dungeon. There was a significant change in his demeanor, too. He seemed to bristle and grow as he adjusted his tie and smoothed back his thick, dark hair.

"Massimiliano," Silvio wheezed, once again struggling against the chains. "I demand to know—"

"Demand?" Max chuckled. "You're hardly in a position to demand anything, Papá."

"No, but I am," Donatella said, finding her feet and inserting herself between her brother and her father.

"Me, too," I added, planting my hands on my hips. "So how about you step away from your father and explain yourself." I'm pretty sure I growled at him, too, but Max merely laughed.

"Was that supposed to intimidate me?" he asked. "Because you know I'm not afraid of you, right?"

I sniffed the air. He wasn't lying. There wasn't so much as a whiff of fear there, only the scent of honey and tobacco, which I presumed was the smell of arrogance. I, on the other hand, probably wreaked of sweat, ammonia, and cat poop—*eau du fear*.

"More fool you," I replied. "Just remember, it didn't take a whole lot of effort to dispense of those vamps, or the werewolf in my kitchen. Kicking your ass won't exactly be a stretch."

"Yes," Max said, turning his attention fully on me. "I heard you dispensed with Beverley quite quickly. Impressive. Mandrillus are particularly hard to kill."

"So I've been told," I replied flatly.

"That's why I sent her after you, you know. Her skill, her kill rate, and her ferocity are legendary."

"*Were* legendary." I smirked. "Now they're just cautionary tales for future lycans to tell their puppies."

"Yes. Well, I don't expect you could even begin to imagine my surprise when I learned you survived not only having your throat torn out, but also being thrown from a third-floor balcony."

"I didn't survive. I died. I just didn't stay dead."

"Hm. So it seems." Max grimaced, like he'd just caught a whiff of dog crap stuck to the bottom of his shoe. He clearly found the thought of my immortality disagreeable. "I didn't believe it at first," he said. "I simply had to see for myself."

"See *what* for yourself?"

I watched Donatella inch her way backward toward Silvio and lay her hand on his chest. His breathing was labored and shallow. She caught my eye, shook her head, and I understood. We didn't have a lot of time to get those chains off him. I mean, I was no rocket scientist, but even I could tell they were causing irreparable damage.

"I had to see Clarissa for myself. That she really was unkillable—the witless recipient of a werewolf heart," he said, grinning at his sister.

"Hey!" I snapped. "Enough with the witless. This is not

going to derail into another, *let's call Clarissa all the crappy names* session."

Donatella frowned. "Vincent explained all this very clearly, Max. What the hell was left to understand?"

Donatella didn't get it, but I did.

And I didn't like it.

Not one bit.

"You knew about me before Vincent said anything."

"Indeed." He nodded.

Donatella's mouth fell slightly open and she blinked at her brother. "What? *How*?"

"So, I gather it was you in the alley behind the Myer Clinic," I said, ignoring Donatella. "You attacked me, and you attacked Nash."

"What alley?" Donatella continued. Her gaze ping-ponging between me and her brother, and then to her father's limp body. At that moment, she looked as desperate and vulnerable as any human I'd ever seen; terrified by the prospect of losing her father, and heartbroken by the realization her brother had betrayed her family in the most horrific way.

I was beginning to see that the familial bonds humans and werewolves both felt weren't all that different to each other.

Love was love was love, apparently, no matter the species.

"I thought I'd finished you off that night." Max shrugged. "Alas, it seems the only person I managed to kill was that useless doctor."

"Bastard," I said, relieved that Max didn't seem to know Nash had survived the alley attack. That was excellent news as far as I was concerned, because that took Nash right off Max's radar. And the fewer people whose wellbeing I had to worry about, the freer I was to deal with him.

"*What doctor*?" Donatella was growing increasingly agitated.

"Oh, do try to keep up, Doni," Max said with a roll of his eyes.

"She really doesn't know, does she?" I asked, pointing at Donatella, but directing my question at Max. Either she really didn't have any clue—join the club—or she was putting on a truly world-class performance. I'm talking, *I'd like to thank the Academy*, worthy.

"And what makes you say that?" Max asked, leering at me. "She could be lying, lulling you into a false sense of security. It's not out of the question."

"No, but I know that's not the case."

"How can you be so sure?"

"Because, 1). I can smell deceit a mile away, and she's not wafting any of those pheromones at the moment. And 2). I'm pretty sure Meryl Streep couldn't top a performance like that if she really was faking."

Max didn't speak or move or blink or anything for a few moments, and I briefly wondered if he'd had a stroke and I just hadn't noticed.

"You'd know, wouldn't you?" he said, eventually. (Nope. No stroke.) "You are, after all, the queen of lies and deception."

I was taken aback. I wasn't deceptive and I definitely wasn't a liar. Okay, well, I never *used* to be a liar. I used to be pretty honest. It wasn't my fault I had to start twisting the truth every five seconds because of all the crazy shit that had been happening to me. If I hadn't made up plausible (although sometimes barely) excuses on the spot, I'd have ended up in the psychiatric ward at Western General on more than one occasion.

So, I was more like an apprentice liar; a liar-in-training.

"You don't agree?" Max asked.

I shook my head. "Of course I don't."

"Alright, then why don't we talk about the performance you and the Peacekeeper put on for the Patrons," Max continued.

He *was* reading my mind!

"That was slippery of Sonny, wasn't it? Pretending to murder you to throw us off the scent, then squirrelling you away from prying eyes."

"Right. Truly diabolical. Hiding me in plain sight like that. Only a real genius could have unraveled that mystery." I shook my head. "Anyone ever tell you your sleuthing skills suck?"

Max sneered. "It was an unconvincing performance at best."

"It felt pretty damn convincing to me," I said, rubbing the spot where Sonny had skewered me. I was still smarting from the physical and emotional wounds inflicted by his betrayal. It would almost certainly leave a scar—because I didn't have enough scars already. Stupid Sonny and stupid Vincent and their stupid, stupid schemes. "Plus, it fooled you, didn't it?"

"Don't be ridiculous," Max said, the side of his mouth curling into an Elvis-esque grin, which sounded a lot sexier than it actually was. "I didn't believe it for a second."

He was totally lying, and I didn't need my werewolf super-senses to smell that bullshit. Max had no idea I was still alive until the moment he'd been flung into the dungeon and saw me with his own two eyes.

I glanced around the room, trying to make a quick assessment of the situation that included throwing together a rough escape plan (PS: there was no escape plan). It was obvious that Sonny wasn't coming to the rescue anytime soon, despite leaving the line open on my mobile so he could hear this ridiculous exchange, so I figured it'd be a good idea to play along, because there was no telling what tasty morsel Max would spill if I just let him talk.

"Okay, I'll bite," I said. "Why are you the only one who figured out Sonny staged my murder, when not even *I* knew about it?"

"Firstly." Max cleared his throat. "You could probably fill a book with all the things you don't know."

Well, that was just rude.

And unnecessary.

Although, true.

Jerk.

"Secondly, I'm a two-hundred-year-old werewolf. I can tell the difference between sterling silver and cheap silver-plate," Max continued. "That dagger was no more dangerous to you than plastic cutlery."

Pfft. Bullshit. I'm pretty sure plastic cutlery wouldn't have stung that badly.

"And thirdly, I've known Sonny for a very long time, and there's no way he would've done anything to hurt you."

"Ha! That's where you're wrong, Mr. *I'm a werewolf. I'm sooooo clever*."

Yep, I mocked him like a school kid.

"Because if you think for a split second Sonny isn't capable of murdering someone, even an innocent someone, to protect and serve the Patrons, let me set you straight. He'd do it in a second. I'm not saying he wouldn't feel bad about it, but—"

"No, no." Max raised his hands. "I know Sonny is capable of carrying out all types of atrocities. I was there for the Lithuanian kalėdinės žudynės. Very bloody," he said with a firm shake of his head.

The bloody Lithuanian what now?

"What I meant was, Sonny wouldn't hurt *you*, specifically. He's grown quite fond of you, but I'm sure you know that."

A little skitter of excitement shot through me knowing there was a pretty good chance Sonny *had* grown fond of me. I knew he had feelings for me, and the prospect of a happily ever after, or even a happy for now, with Sonny, no longer scared me. In fact, it had the opposite effect.

Mine.

Forever.

And ever.

And there it was. I guess my heart really had chosen Sonny as my life mate. Well, whaddayaknow.

"Not that I blame him," Max continued. I'd almost forgotten he was there. "If there were ever a woman who could distract me from my life's work," he reached out and traced the back of his fingers down my arm, "it'd be you."

I smacked his hand away.

"Listen here, buddy," I barked. "There never was, nor will there ever be, any distracting of anyone's life work now, or in the future, so get that straight."

"If you say so," Max said in a tone so smarmy, I wanted to snap his nose off and shove it up his—well, you know where.

"Also," I continued. "And please let me make this crystal clear, if you ever touch me again, even by accident, I promise I will rip your arm off and beat you with the bloody stump. *Comprende?*"

Max quirked a brow, but eventually nodded. "Certainly."

I'd heard election promises that were more convincing, but it wasn't the time to labor my point. I'd done my due diligence, now it was all up to him. If he touched me again, they'd be calling him *Leftie* down at the Werewolf Country Club for the rest of his crappy life.

"Max," Silvio coughed. "Explain yourself *immediatamente*." He was not sounding good, and he was looking pretty shabby as well.

Max rolled his eyes and leaned toward me. "That's so typical of him, you know? Always impatient. Never interested in hearing what others have to say."

"Wow, talk about the narcissist calling the kettle selfish," I murmured, but predictably, Max didn't even acknowledge I'd spoken.

"Well, now you're going to wait, Papá. You're going to listen to *me*, if it's the last thing you do." Max snickered, like the giant loser he was. "Actually, it *will* be the last thing you do, but I presume you're not in a rush to die, are you?"

Silvio looked crestfallen and I felt a pang in my heart at the sight of this great man so stricken.

"I thought as much. So, why don't you shut your mouth and I'll let you live...for now. Miss Hunt and I have business to attend to, don't we?"

"If you say so." I shrugged. "Does it involve speeding things along? Because I'm with your old man...this is taking forever. I mean, I know you love the sound of your own voice, but to the rest of us, it's like a fingernails-down-a-chalkboard situation." I grinned at him, but felt no amusement.

"Fine. I'll get to the point. I'm tired of you all, anyway." He clapped his hands and rubbed his palms together. "Tell me, Clarissa, why do you think humans are the most dominant race on the earth?" Max screwed up his nose when he said *humans*, like someone had let a fart slip in a crowded elevator. "Why are they the apex predators, when we all know the lycans are far more powerful, potent and intelligent?"

"I can't say I've ever—"

"I mean even surely you, knowing what you now know, must understand just how beyond ridiculous that is?"

"You know what sounds beyond ridiculous to me? You and your incessant prattling," I jibed. "I'm so bored right now, I'm beginning to wish I actually *was* dead."

Max bared his teeth and growled at me. "You might want to start showing a little more respect, or you might regret it," he said.

"Oh, I already regret this whole thing." I sighed. "Fine. I'll play. Why are humans the dominant race? Um, is it because we're resilient; inquisitive and ambitious? Maybe it's because we're empathetic, and—"

"No," Max interrupted.

I raised my brows. "We're not empathetic?"

Max shrugged. "I don't know and I don't care. Humans rule the world because we *let them*," he said.

"Who lets them?"

"The paranormals. Those of us who dwell in the Inner World. We just accept the way things are; the way they've been since the stupid Patrons came along and ruined everything."

Batten down the hatches. I could feel a rant coming on.

"We have been played for fools, spending most of our time bickering amongst ourselves; expending far too much energy on petty squabbles, rather than focusing on the actual problem."

"And that would be?"

"Lack of strong leadership." He puffed out his chest. "Someone who understands the old ways but isn't afraid to adapt…or stand up and take charge, at any price."

I rubbed my eyes with the heels of my hands. "So, what, you negotiated a treaty with the vampires to take over the world, and convinced them to put a Blood Bounty on my head?"

Max shrugged. "The Bounty was their idea. I merely funded it."

Rude.

"But why?"

"To get rid of the evidence, of course." He crossed his arms.

"Okay, I've just about had enough. What in the hell are the two of you talking about?" Donatella raged. "Just stop. Stop talking in circles and explain what the hell is going on. What *evidence*?"

"He's talking about me, Donatella. I'm the evidence," I said.

"Evidence of *what*?" Her glare snapped to her brother. "One of you better tell me what's going on, right now!"

I eyed Max.

"Would you like to tell her, or shall I?" he asked.

I knew he was dying to spill his guts. No way was he going to miss the opportunity to gloat in front of his big sister and father.

"Be my guest," I said, gesturing at Donatella.

Max leaned closer to his sister. "Evidence that I had our brother murdered. How's that, sister? Clear enough for you?"

I heard both Silvio and Donatella gasp, but didn't dare look at either of them. Max was confessing everything now, and I wasn't about to do anything to ruin his rant.

"I don't believe you," Donatella growled. "You're a liar."

"Am I?" Max said, crossing his arms and rocking back and forth on his heels like the gigantic smug bastard he was. "I'm a lot of things, but I'm not a liar. You know that."

"Why?" Donatella sobbed and squeaked; her throat tight, strangling her words before they could even be spoken. "Why would you do this?"

"Why? *Why?*" Max's arm shot out, and he pointed an accusatory finger at his father. "Because of him."

"Me?" Silvio recoiled. "What did I do?"

"You ruined *EVERYTHING*! You turned us into a laughing stock!" Max was in full rant mode now, all bulging veins and spittle flying…and he was oozing some of the grossest pheromones I'd ever smelled. "Once upon a time, we were warriors—feared, loathed by all species. And we were utterly invincible. Now, we're lap dogs to humans. We cower and we compromise and we grovel. And it's all your fault."

Someone had serious daddy issues.

"All your talk of peaceful coexistence, of collaboration…you make me sick! I had to do something about it," Max roared. "But my ambitions were never going to be realized while I was bound by the antiquated, and might I add, completely unreasonable, rules of succession upheld by *you*."

"What rules might that be?" I asked.

"Birthright."

I frowned. "Like a monarchy? I mean, I'm no royalist, but I've watched enough episodes of *The Crown* to know how these things work…ish."

"Birthright is a ridiculous concept," Max continued. "I am stronger, smarter, and more powerful than Dante ever was. Yet, he was being groomed to be alpha, purely because he was born first. Unacceptable."

Max was flapping his arms around so much, I thought he was going to fly off. Maybe he was? Do werewolves fly? Do they have wings or built in jet packs? I sighed and filed the questions in the 'More Weird Shit to Google' part of my brain.

If anyone should be angry about birthright and succession, it should be me," Donatella chimed in. "I'm the eldest, but can I become alpha? Nope. And you know why? Because I'm female."

"I have to say," I interjected, nodding at Donatella. "That's so unfair."

She offered me a tiny smile.

"But I'd never be so incredibly insane, as to kill my own brother in cold blood."

"Actually, I didn't kill him. I outsourced," Max said, massaging his forehead with his fingertips.

"To the *vampires*?" I asked.

Max shrugged. At least he had the decency to look sheepish.

"I thought werewolves hated vampires. Actually I thought *everyone* hated vampires."

"Oh, we do. But I didn't want Dante's untimely demise tied back to me, and no one would ever have suspected that a werewolf would collude with vampires. It all would have gone to plan, too—"

"If it weren't for those meddling kids?" I interjected.

No one laughed but me. Cleary no *Scooby Doo* fans here.

"But I overestimated their competence…and intellect. Now I realize I should have done things myself because if I had, we wouldn't be in this predicament now, would we?"

"And what predicament would that be?" Donatella asked.

"This one," he said, pointing to my transplant scar.

I glared at him, and crossed my arms over my chest. "You're the reason I got mixed up in all this."

"I guess so..." he said, "...in a way. Yes, I'm the one who hired the vampires to kill Dante, but I played no part in what they did with him afterward."

"Which was what exactly?"

"Isn't it obvious? They sold off his remains on the black market, which was not at all what I had in mind when I told them to get rid of him. I was thinking more garbage disposal or bonfire."

There was another gasp from both Donatella and Silvio, but if Max heard them, he didn't acknowledge it.

"I know, I know. I should have overseen the disposal of his remains myself. Actually, I should have just lopped his head off with Papá's broadsword and eaten his remains...but I didn't."

My stomach churned. So gross.

"What? *Why*?" Donatella spluttered.

"The vital organs of paranormal creatures fetch a pretty penny on the black market," Max replied.

He wasn't lying about that. I'd seen it for myself on the dark web. Shaman, Kadji, voodoo practitioners—they all use them for potions and charms, fertility spells...*resurrections*.

"And it seems the lure of making fast money was far too great for the *sanguisugi*. Morons that they are." He rolled his eyes. "But, in their defense, it's not like any of us had any idea someone was Frankensteining organs and transplanting them into humans. I, for one, didn't even know it was possible."

"You and me both," I replied. "So, what's the going rate for werewolf leftovers, anyway?"

"It varies. Vital organs, like the kidneys, liver, brain and lungs, we're talking six-figures—*high* six-figures. Non-vital organs, gallbladder, pancreas, stomach...mid-five figures. And for the smaller stuff, the reproductive system, sensory organs, lobes and glands, they can go for low five-figures."

My throat tightened, my mouth went dry and my chest felt like it was going to explode. "What…what about a heart?" I asked. "What are they worth?"

"Seven to eight figures, depending on the breed." He smirked. "Some are more valuable than others."

Max looked at me closely, too closely for my liking. He made my skin crawl, especially with that smarmy look on his face. "*Someone* invested a lot of money in you."

Donatella growled and bared her teeth. "You're a disgrace," she said.

"Yes, well you would say that. You're just as pathetic as Papá."

"Massimiliano, tell me it's not true," Silvio begged. "Tell me you didn't kill your brother, then desecrate his body."

"*Oh, for God's sake*! I told you, Papá, I didn't kill him. The vampires did, and then they sold him off like yesterday's trash." Max threw his hands in the air. "See what I mean," he said, turning to me. "He never listens."

"Your own flesh and blood?" Silvio whimpered.

"Dante meant nothing to me." The veins in Max's neck and temples bulged and pulsed, and the stench of rotting apples and peroxide wafted from him. *Ick*. "He was merely the thing standing between me and what I wanted; to be your heir."

"You're not half the man he was," Donatella sneered.

"No, but I'm twice the werewolf." Max sprang forward, lunging at his sister and backhanding her so hard, she flew ten feet backward, slamming heavily against the bluestone wall. Plumes of masonry dust swirled in the air as her body plopped limply on the cold, stone floor.

"*Disgrazia*," Silvio growled, stumbling to his knees. "I wish you had never been born. If I could, I'd kill you myself."

"But you can't, can you, Papá?" Max taunted. "Because you're weak and pathetic, just like your precious Dante."

Silvio's eyes narrowed and, to my simultaneous delight and horror, he spat on Max's Versace loafers.

Good for him.

Also, *yuck*.

Max didn't seem to echo my sentiments though, shoving Silvio to the ground and swiftly kicking him in the ribs, twice.

"What do you have to say now, Papá?"

Silvio gasped. "You murdered my son. I have nothing to say."

Max grabbed Silvio by the collar and yanked him back to his feet. "I'm your son, too!" Max screamed so loud, his words rattled and bounced around the cavernous room.

"You have two sons, Papá. *Two*." Max was near hysterics. "Well, you *had* two. Now there's just me."

Silvio didn't reply. He merely cradled his head and sobbed.

Max threw his father back to the ground and wiped Donatella's blood from the back of his hand.

"You really are a dick, you know that, right?" I said.

Max sobered. "I'd watch what I say if I were you, Miss Hunt."

"Or what?" I asked. "You gonna kill me?"

Max produced a silver dagger from beneath his jacket. That'll serve me right for opening my big trap.

"You know I was kidding about the killing part, right?" I backpedaled. "I'm sure we can work something out."

Max's face split into a wide grin. "Oh, we'll work something out, alright," he said. "But first—"

Max spun around so quickly, he was little more than a blur. In fact, I'm pretty sure the only reason I'd been able to follow his movements at all was because of my werewolf superpowers. He flipped the dagger in the air, catching it by the blade, and threw it at Silvio. The dagger spun through the air before plunging deep into his father's chest, all the way to the hilt. Silvio's bloodcurdling howl turned my blood to ice and I watched in horror as he slumped forward and crumpled to the ground.

Without missing a beat, Max wrenched the dagger from his father's chest, spun again and plunged it straight into Donatella's ribcage. She didn't see it coming. Neither had I.

It's not often I'm rendered speechless.

It was a very strange sensation.

"Don't worry, I'll make sure no one sells their body parts on the black market," he said, turning to me and tapping the side of his head. "I've learned my lesson."

Something primal stirred deep inside me. White-hot rage boiling in my veins.

"Look at you," Max said, wiping Silvio's and Donatella's blood from the blade with his index finger and thumb and flicking the ruby droplets to the floor. "All puffed up and angry. I like it. Very becoming."

"You won't get away with this," I snarled.

Max simply smirked and glanced at the crumpled bodies of his sister and father. "Seems like I already have."

"You might have the upper hand right now, but I promise, I will destroy you. I will destroy you for all you have done to this family. I will avenge our father. I will avenge my death. I will rip your still-beating heart out,"

Wait. *What the hell did I just say?*

Max threw back his head and howled.

What the hell was that about? And what had I said? Avenge my death? *My* death? I wasn't dead…for once. Not at that moment, anyway.

"And, *there* you are," Max said, grinning from ear to ear. "I've been waiting for you, brother."

"I don't know what you're talking about," I replied, my stomach sinking to my feet. "I meant to say Dante's death. I will avenge *Dante's* death."

"You said exactly what you meant say. I knew some part of

him had to be lurking in there somewhere. I just had to flush him out."

Panic. Attack. Eminent.

"All it took was a little prodding."

"No one is lurking anywhere," I snapped. "It was a slip of the tongue. Nothing more."

What.

The.

Fuuuuuuuuuck!

Despite my escalating terror and crippling anxiety, I had to keep a cool head, otherwise I'd be the next to get skewered and I was in no rush to relive that experience.

Max brushed his palms together, as if he were wiping away the grime of a hard day's work. He was still grinning like an idiot and I was trying very hard not to slap the stupid smile off his face.

"You can say whatever you want to help you get through this, but we both know the truth," Max said. "The question is, what do I do with you now, Clarissa?" He tapped his lips with the tip of his index finger. "On one hand, you stand between me and my rightful place as alpha."

"I'm not standing in the way of anything," I responded.

"So, the decision to eliminate you *should* be easy."

"But it's not?"

"Surprisingly, no. This whole situation is quite unexpected and has me perplexed. You see, Vincent and Sonny seem to have taken quite a shine to you. Vincent has made it very clear you are not to be touched."

"Was that before or after he and Sonny murdered me?"

"Before. Ironically." Max smirked. "And his orders were very specific; no harm should come to you, not so much as a hair on your head should be touched, or the consequences would be swift and final."

"You mean like, excommunication?" I asked.

"No. I mean like, death. So, making the decision to kill you hasn't been easy."

"Small mercies."

"Now I'm faced with the $64,000 Question: do I kill you, permanently this time, of course, and risk Vincent and Sonny's wrath if they were to find out? Or might there be another way?"

Ooh, ooh! I know the answer to this. Another way! There was another way!

If only I could think what the other way might be. Which, of course, I couldn't. Why would I? It's not like I was in the habit of talking people out of killing me. These days, I just got killed and that was that. This was the first time I'd been given the opportunity to negotiate, not that I was doing a good job of it.

So what did that leave me with? Not much, except doing what I did best: talking until something useful came out, or he got fed up and just killed me.

I took a deep breath. "Look, I don't even know why this is a problem," I said. "Clearly being alpha is super-important to you, and why wouldn't it be? All those plebs to boss around and torture and whatnot," I wheezed. (I was still recovering from the shock of my little split personality episode earlier. I was feeling very Sybil.) "I don't want to be alpha."

"I'm afraid you don't have a choice. You carry my dead brother's heart. The *heir's* heart. While it still beats, I cannot be alpha."

"You can be alpha. I don't want any part of any of it. No one needs to know about my heart. Not Sonny. Not Vincent. No one. I won't even so much as whisper about, you know…" I pointed at my transplant scar.

"I wish I could believe you."

"You can totally believe me. I'm an excellent secret-keeper. I'm practically a vault. My friends, they all call me Fort Knox."

"Really?" Max said, crossing his arms over his chest.

"No. But that doesn't mean I can't keep a secret. I can even give you an example. Um, okay. My cousin, Regina, told me she's been having an affair with our other cousin Bianca's husband, Carl, for like a year. Totally swore me to secrecy." I buttoned my mouth to illustrate just how tightlipped I could be. "I haven't told a single soul about it...until now, that is." I cringed, realizing that I'd just revealed a secret while I was trying to demonstrate how well I could keep a secret secret. *Urgh*. No wonder I kept getting killed. "But, before you do something drastic, let me reiterate that, up until right now, I haven't mentioned a word of it to anyone."

"And just how long has that been?"

"Um..." I stopped and counted on my fingers. "About five weeks-ish," I said.

"My, my, five whole weeks. Personal best?"

"Kind of," I conceded.

"I'm afraid I'd want a guarantee of silence that lasted much longer than a month, Clarissa."

"Well, obviously I'd make a lot more effort to keep your secret than I did Regina's," I replied. "Who even cares that she's pregnant with Carl's kid, anyway? No one. Except Bianca, maybe. But your secret, that's a doozy. I wouldn't utter a word about it."

He smiled, a big, toothy grin, and if I didn't know better, I'd say his teeth had, I don't know, multiplied, somehow. Was this guy a Great White shifter, too? Because he looked freaky weird.

"You know, I can completely understand why Vincent and Sonny are so enamored with you," Max said. "You have a certain quality."

"Sparkling personality? Sharp mind? Brilliant sense of humor?" I suggested.

"Childish charm."

"Oh."

#deflated

"You know," Max said, angling toward me. He spun the

silver dagger in the palm of his hand before pulling a white handkerchief from his breast pocket and rubbing down the grip. "I think you just might have some potential, Miss Hunt. But first—"

Max grabbed my arm and yanked me forward. I braced myself for the excruciating sensation of the blade plunging into my heart, but instead he slapped the dagger into my hand and wrapped my fingers around the grip.

"What? What's this?" I asked, puzzled.

"Insurance," he said, using the handkerchief to pluck the dagger from my hand. He held it in front of me. "Now, I have your fingerprints on the weapon that killed my sister and my father. We wouldn't want it ending up in the hands of the police, now would we?"

I gaped at him. "You're diabolical."

"Thank you," he said, dropping the dagger into a baggie and sealing the top. "I do try."

"You do know what diabolical means, right?"

Max smiled tightly, but didn't bother answering me. "Personally, I find that partnerships work so much better when each party has something to lose. Don't you?"

"Would it even matter if I didn't?"

He really was a genius. He was also completely insane and psychologically challenged, but a genius nonetheless.

"Now, I feel like we can move forward. You keep my little indiscretions secret, and I'll ensure this dagger never sees the light of day. Deal?" Max extended his hand.

As I saw it, I had little choice. Max was clearly willing to do anything to become alpha, not least of which, slaughtering his entire family. He wouldn't bat an eye if he had to frame me for murder. I had the option of fighting him there and then, and hoping I still had enough juice left in the tank to kick his ass. But, I didn't like my chances. And I couldn't get justice for Silvio or Donatella or Dante if I were dead, and I certainly couldn't do it if I were in prison for their murders. The only chance I had was making a deal with Max, then using whatever resources I had at my disposal to retrieve the knife, then exposing him.

Easy peasy.

Not.

"Don't leave me hanging," Max said, regaining my attention. "Do we have a deal?"

I looked down at Max's proffered hand, raised mine and slipped it into his.

It was clammy and cold.

Yuck.

"To new partnerships," Max said. "I have a feeling about this."

"So do I," I replied. "Say, you don't happen to have any Kwells on you, per chance?"

Promising myself I'd do everything I could to right the wrongs Max had committed against his family, I shook his hand, and fought the nagging feeling I'd just sold my soul to the devil.

TWELVE

I'M NOT SURE WHAT HAPPENED FIRST, the west-facing wall blowing *out*. The internal oak door exploding *in*. Donatella bursting to life and charging at Max. Or two-dozen *gnomes* storming the dungeon, screaming like teeny, tiny banshees. It was like being invaded by Christmas decorations.

Whatever the catalyst, it set off a chain reaction resulting in bedlam the likes of which I'd never seen. And I'd queued for twelve-hours at the Boxing Day sales at Chaddie. Twice.

The dungeon was, for all intents and purposes, obliterated. Chunks of basalt and red brick, oak splinters, and shrapnel rocketed in all directions, scattering rubble and debris everywhere. Thick clouds of acrid, choking smoke (which may or may not have been tear gas) quickly filled the room, and concrete dust and wreckage blanketed everything including, but not limited to, my hair, lips, eyelashes, throat, clothing, and every other bodily crevice imaginable.

#itchy

#scratchy

#notcomfy

Despite the mayhem and confusion, the most surprising thing wasn't either of the explosions, or the teeny, tiny warriors flipping around like mini super-ninjas, but rather Donatella springing to life and attacking her brother like a woman possessed.

As it turns out, Max completely missed Donatella's heart

when he'd stabbed her, instead only puncturing her lung, which is the lycan equivalent of a paper cut.

Epic. Werewolf. Fail.

She'd obviously bided her time, waiting for the right moment (somewhere around the time the wall and door exploded) to attack, and when she did, wow, was it epic.

Seeing two impeccably manicured people transform into frothing, snarling, drooly werewolves was something I knew I'd never forget. Like I knew I wouldn't forget the unmistakable sound of tearing flesh, cracking bones, and snapping tendons as the change took hold—mainly because it had already been indelibly imprinted on my memory after the whole Beverley thing.

Once the fight was in full swing, it was like being in the middle of an *Ultimate Fighter* smack down. Blood and bits e-v-e-r-y-w-h-e-r-e. Fur flew, razor-sharp claws flashed, and fangs gnashed. It was pure pandemonium.

And the roaring; the roaring and growling and snarling and howling was deafening. It was terrifying and exhilarating and shocking and fascinating and...well, mostly, it was just terrifying.

In the spirit of girl power, and female solidarity, and the sisterhood, (but really, just because I wanted to clip the guy responsible for ruining my life), I did my best to back Donatella up. In my own unique, clumsy way. I picked up the heaviest object I could lay my mitts on—a hefty section of the shattered oak door—and beaned *someone* in the head with it. I *think* it was Max. I *hoped* it was Max. But I couldn't be sure.

Whoever it was, I clocked them just before I got blindsided by a stray block of basalt that knocked me clear off my feet and sent me sailing across the rubble.

And once again, everything went black.

Lights out.

When I woke up, I was in hospital (again... *urgh*), but I

wasn't alone. Azrael, Sonny, and Nash were all standing at the foot of my bed, peering at me like I was an exhibit at The Lume.

"Am I dead?" I asked, my voice croaky, my throat dry.

"No," Azrael replied, his brow creased.

"Am I in some sort of life-threatening danger?"

Sonny shook his head.

"So, I'm sick, then?"

"Not really," Nash replied. "You have a few injuries, but nothing critical—"

"Then, why are you all here?"

The Three Weird Amigos looked at each other, then back at me.

"We're just visiting," Nash said, with a shrug.

"At the same time?" I asked.

"I was here first," Sonny said, puffing out his impressive chest.

Azrael rolled his eyes. "Oh please."

"I was," Sonny insisted. "I saved your life, Clarissa."

"And she cracked you over the head with a door, for your troubles," Azrael muttered.

Okay, so I guess it wasn't Max I clipped.

"I think you'll find the doctors saved her life," Nash said, clearing his throat. "And I stitched up your head."

Sonny scowled at both of them but didn't utter another word.

I tried to hoist myself up into a sitting position, but the pain that shot from my shoulder up the back of my neck and finally to my head, only just stopped short of knocking me out. I flopped back against the lumpy, bumpy hospital pillows, and winced.

"You need to take it easy," Nash said, stepping forward and brushing his hand along my arm, which I'm sure was as much a reassuring gesture as it was his usual bedside manner. It was really sweet, though, and I smiled in appreciation.

"How about you step away from her, Doc?" Sonny said, crossing his arms.

Testosterone alert, anyone?

"Well, given I'm the only one in the room with a medical degree, and she's clearly in some physical distress, it's my responsibility to monitor her."

"Are you her doctor?" Azrael asked.

"Well, no," Nash replied.

"Then, if anyone's doing any monitoring, it'll be me," Sonny said.

"Um, you know I can hear you, right?" I said.

"Oh, so you're going to check her oxygen levels, are you?" Nash said, ignoring me. "How about her sutures? Monitor for signs of infection? What about her pain medication? Would you like to adjust that?"

"How about I adjust your nose?"

"Hello! I'm right here," I yelled, swatting Nash away, and glaring at Sonny. "Don't talk about me like I'm in a coma unless I'm in a coma. Wait, I'm not in a coma, am I?"

"No," Nash said.

"In that case, stop talking *about* me, and start talking *to* me."

At least they all had the decency to look sheepish.

"So, Dr Nash." I glared at Sonny, just in case he had any ideas about inserting himself further into the conversation. "What's the sitch?"

Nash stepped closer to me and smirked at Sonny.

FFS.

"Don't make me regret asking you," I warned.

He shook his head. "I won't."

"Thank you," I said. "Well?"

"Right. So, you've got a few bumps and grazes, a nasty contusion here." Nash pointed to the right side of my head. "And a sizable lump on the back of your skull they're keeping an eye on for a hematoma, plus significant shoulder damage."

"That's from yanking Silvio's chain," I explained.

"Pardon? You yanked Silvio's chain? That's not a euphemism, is it?"

"Don't be disgusting, Sonny," Azrael barked before slugging him in the shoulder. It took all my willpower not to send them both to the naughty corner.

"Anyway," Nash continued, tossing Sonny some serious stink eye. "What they're actually really interested in the rate at which you're healing—highly accelerated. We know that's a byproduct of your werewolf heart, but for them, it's intriguing. It's drawing attention, which I presume you're trying to avoid."

Azrael baulked, twitched, glared at Nash, glared at Sonny, and glared at *me*. Was he having a seizure? He then pulled a small crossbow, of all things, from under his coat, crouched and scoured the room like he was preparing for an ambush. Definitely some kind of seizure.

"What are you doing?" I asked.

"Checking."

"For what?"

"To see if anyone's listening to the Doc here talk about…" He glanced around again. "*W.E.R.E.W.O.L.V.E.S.*"

"Why are you spelling it out?" I asked.

"Because it's top secret."

"And you really think the doctors and nurses wouldn't be able to break your sophisticated spelling code which, by the way, I'm pretty sure a fourth-grader could crack?"

Azrael scowled at me, then pointed to my chest. "Why does he know about, about… You know?"

"My boobies?" I asked, grinning. I loved seeing him squirm. It was one of the few joys I had in life at that moment.

"What? No," Azrael replied, squirming.

Ahhhh, sweet success.

"Don't worry, the doc knows everything," Sonny said.

"Not about her boobies, I don't," Nash grumbled.

"You better not." Sonny glared at Nash. "But he does know

about the transplant, the Patrons, werewolves, the Inner World," Sonny explained. "The whole shebang."

"What? How? Why'd you do that?" Azrael shrieked. "Why'd you tell him?"

"Hey, don't shoot the messenger, Big Fella. I didn't tell him anything," Sonny said, pointing at me. "*She* told him. I was just as annoyed as you when I found out."

"I'm not a complete imbecile, you know?" Nash said, planting his hands on his hips.

"That's debatable," Sonny mumbled.

"I worked out something was wrong after I was mauled by the werewolf in the alley."

"That was Max," I said. "Max De Benedetto." But none of them were listening.

"And how *did* you survive that, Doc?" Sonny quizzed, scratching the whiskers on his chin with the tips of his fingers. "I heard you were in pretty bad shape."

"You believe everything you hear?" Nash replied.

I cleared my throat. "Again," I said. "I'm *right here, people.* Can we stay focused?"

"Sorry. Sorry," they muttered. "Won't happen again. Sorry."

"That's better," I said. "Now, can you please tell me what the hell happened, and how I ended up here with you fools bickering and gawking at me like I'm some sideshow attraction?"

Of course, they did the exact opposite of what I wanted, and all shouted at me at once.

"... you helped me realize someone was trying to eliminate the De Benedettos..."... Vincent got to work locating you..."

"... vampires' nest at the old asylum in Sunbury..."

"... of course, I didn't have my car because it had been impounded..."

"... doing my evening rounds when you were brought in..."

"... deployed the First Gnome Infantry..."

"... C4 detonators around the exterior wall and main door..."

"… I pulled a few strings to access your file…"

"… one casualty, a lycan, but have yet to formally identify the remains…"

"… Emergency Services brought you here…"

"… two police officers have been reported missing…"

"… two cases might be related…"

"… taking care of the witnesses…"

I could make out neither hide nor hair of what they were talking about and felt like my head was going to explode. There was so much noise—loud, loud noise, like everyone in the world was in my head, yelling at me, and I couldn't distinguish one voice from the other.

I pressed the heels of my hands into my eyes and clenched my teeth. "Stop. Just stop. All you're doing is annoying me," I snapped. "One of you tell me the story, start to finish, and the other two, shoosh."

Of course, they started talking over the top of each other again, and I was this close to clunking their heads together like they were the Three Stooges.

What kind of stupid were they, anyway? Magical? Genetic? Environmental? Sociological? Maybe they were just naturally stupid.

"Okay, that's enough. Shut up, all of you."

There were a few more murmurs but they all quieted once they realized I had my angry face on. Unbeknownst to them, it wasn't just my angry face. It was also my *I'm in pain* face, my tired face, and my *so fed up I could cry* face, mixed in with a touch of everyone's favorite, my premenstrual face.

They were all pretty similar.

I was sore all over, had a care factor of zero, and just wanted to know what the hell had happened.

I also wanted to sleep.

A lot.

Like, for days.

I looked at Nash. "Can I have something for the pain?"

He nodded and pointed to the patient-controlled analgesia pump lying near my left hand. "Press the red button."

"What is it?"

"Most likely morphine or hydromorphone. It'll administer a measured dose, for your comfort."

I pressed the red button. Twice.

It only took a few minutes for the medication to kick in, making my head feel foggy and my limbs heavy. It wasn't the most pleasant of sensations (I much preferred Prince Valium), but it was better than being in pain.

My eyelids were like lead, my sight grew dim, and my body felt… I guess fat would be the best way to describe it. "*Whennnn I wake uuuup,*" I slurred. "Only *onnne offff* you better be *hhhh-herrrrre.*"

"Which one?" Azrael asked.

"*Sssssssonny,*" I replied just before I passed out.

Maybe morphine wasn't so bad after all.

THIRTEEN

"I DIDN'T KILL MAX," I protested. "At least, I don't think I did."

When I woke up, Sonny wasn't in my room, but Vincent was, which wasn't entirely bad. We hadn't exactly spent much time together of late, mainly because every time we did, things ended with me screeching at him for betraying me, or for colluding with Sonny to kill me, or for revealing some morbid secret I could happily have gone my entire life without ever knowing. But that's what you get when you hang out with the head of a super-secret organization that controls the paranormal world. It's not a normal friendship.

In his defense, it's not like Vincent was all that accustomed to making new friends, not human ones anyway. Nor was he exactly forthcoming with the truth, for obvious reasons. Still, I was glad it was him and not the other three knuckleheads who had been there earlier, because having Sonny, Azrael, and Nash all yammering at me at once made me want to stab myself in the ears with sharpened chopsticks just so I wouldn't have to listen to them.

Vincent, however—handsome, patient, wise, elegant, Vincent (I may or may not have still been under the influence of the morphine)—had done exactly what I'd wanted. He explained what the hell had happened in the dungeon and how I'd ended up in hospital with yet another concussion. According to *him*, he'd used his Pictish skills of divination to locate me after I'd been kidnapped. (I called bullshit on that. I'd have bet a year of smashed avo toasts that Rebecca helped Sonny use the FINDME app I'd installed on his phone to pinpoint my location. Modern technology came to my rescue, not his supernatural powers. Divination, my butt.)

After they figured out exactly where I was, Vincent ordered the vampire nest be destroyed by the Gnome Army. Yep. Gnome. Army. (Mental note: Gnome Army? WTF? Ask Sonny to explain that freak show.)

Aaaaand, long story short, we were all saved.

Well, some of us were saved.

Others of us were minced meat.

"It certainly looks like your handiwork," Vincent continued. "His head was torn off, and his spine ripped out. All the way down the coccyx."

"That does sound like me," I said, gnawing on my fingernail, which was no mean feat given I'd only had my shellac redone the week before. It was like chewing through fiberglass. "But I don't remember doing it. Wouldn't I remember? I remember the others." I was as much talking to myself as I was talking to Vincent at that point. "Beverley, the vampire henchmen, Constable Brown."

"Constable Brown?"

"What did Donatella say? Did she actually say I killed Max?"

"She didn't say much. We didn't have the chance to speak to her before she—"

"Before she *what*? She didn't die, did she?" Panic. Attack. Eminent.

"No, Miss Jump to Conclusions. If you let me finish, we didn't have the chance to speak to her before she was taken into recovery by her pack. Lycans have very specific methods of healing their sick and injured. Their traditions are based just as much in ritual, spirituality, and magicks as they are in blood and brutality."

"Could have fooled me." I hadn't seen much spirituality in my dealings with werewolves. I'd seen a lot of biting, scratching, ripping stuff up—and drool, so much drool—but spirituality? Yeah, nah.

"And it seems Donatella needs all the help she can get. She's in a terrible state. Her injuries are, well, devastating. It's a miracle she survived at all."

I felt the prick of hot tears sting the backs of my eyes. "Did I… Did I do that to her?"

Vincent reached out and patted my arm in a stilted, *there, there, there, there,* motion. It was ridiculously robotic, yet strangely comforting. "I was hoping you could tell me, but if you can't, it's understandable. You're confused and exhausted. Try not to get worked up."

Easy for him to say. He was used to killing things. I was not. Although, it was becoming obvious I'd have to make peace with it sooner rather than later.

"I'm sure once you recover, you'll start to remember—"

"Remember what? How I murdered Max? And might have also murdered Donatella? No thank you." I was crying by that stage. Ugly crying. I bet I looked like a panda… A panda covered in tears and snot. Yuck. "Or maybe I'll remember how I turned into some bloodthirsty freak, and maimed and killed innocent people—"

"I wouldn't exactly call Max innocent. Or people, for that matter."

"Is that really the point?" I frowned.

"A little." Vincent shrugged. "No. Not really. But I'm sure if you did attack and kill Max, and that's a big *IF*, there must have been a valid reason."

"Of course there was a valid reason," I sniped. "You should know me well enough to know I'm not in the habit of killing people for shits and giggles. Max was a nutjob and if I was the one who killed him, it's because he deserved it," I raged. "None of this would even have happened if he wasn't such a power-hungry megalomaniac. Who even murders their own brother then sells his body parts on the black market? *Who*?"

"I beg your pardon?" Vincent spluttered. "Max did *what*?"

"You know, Max killed Dante so he could become heir, but then he sold his organs on the black market, and some of them ended up in, well, me." I pointed to my chest. "Then he planned to kill Silvio so he could become alpha. *Shit*, Silvio. Is he okay? I mean, is he alive?"

Vincent stood and paced the room, running his hands through his lush, dark locks. "Are you sure?"

"Am I sure about what?" I asked.

"That Max killed Dante and sold off his vital organs."

I snort-laughed. "Positive. I might not remember what happened *after* the concussion, but I remember everything that happened before. He's the reason I'm in this crazy mess in the first place."

"This is unbelievable," Vincent grumbled. "How did we miss this? I'm a Seer, for heaven's sake. A *Seer*. And Sonny, he's a… He's a…"

I gaped with giddy anticipation. "Sonny's a what? A merman? A djinn? A Titan? *What*? What is he?"

Vincent exhaled, long and deep, and centered himself. "Sonny is a Peacekeeper."

I rolled my eyes. "Ripped off." I was never going to find out what the hell Sonny was. Which was completely unfair, especially given he was supposedly my life mate.

"We have intelligence on every continent, in every country, from every species. I'm an immortal for heaven's sake! How could this have happened right under my nose?"

Wowsers. Someone was losing control and losing it fast. I had to stop this crazy train before it completely derailed.

"Look. I know all this is bad, like super bad. But, you know what else would be super bad? Silvio being dead."

Vincent stopped pacing and scrubbed his hands down his face. He wasn't listening to me. He was off in his own little world of confusion and paranoia. It was a place I was quite familiar with.

"Vincent!" I snapped my fingers to get his attention. "Is Silvio alive?"

Vincent looked up at me with a vague, faraway look in his eyes. "Excuse me? Oh, Silvio. No."

"*What*?"

"What? Oh, sorry. I mean, yes. He's alive. He's recovering."

"Oh, for pity's sake, are you trying to give me a heart attack?"

"I don't think you can actually have one anymore," he said with that puzzled puppy look on his face, again.

"Felt like a bloody heart attack," I grumbled, rubbing the spot on my chest that had exploded with white-hot pain the moment I thought Silvio was dead. That was clearly going to take some getting used to.

"How did Silvio survive, though? The stabbing, I mean," I asked, frantically pressing the red button on the analgesia pump, hoping to get a little pain relief for the shiny, new sore spot I'd developed in the middle of my chest.

But nothing happened.

No pain relief for Clarissa.

Poop.

"What stabbing?" Vincent asked, stepping closer to my bed.

"Max stabbed Silvio with a silver dagger. Which, by the way, I'm beginning to think isn't half as lethal as *someone* would have had me believe—"

"He did *what*?"

I eyed Vincent. He was becoming screechy and agitated. His neck was all blotchy and—wait...was he *sweating*? What the hell?

I cleared my throat. "Max stabbed Silvio in the chest with a silver dagger. You need to pay closer attention."

"I *am* paying attention! But you're talking in circles, just for something different."

Geez, talk about the pot calling the kettle black. He was always talking in circles, Vincent was the giant circle-talkerer, not me. I chose straight talk only.

Okay, so maybe I didn't always choose straight talk. There was a tiny possibility I hadn't made myself entirely clear when I'd started telling him about the Max situation. I do have a propensity for starting conversations halfway through. There might have been a circle or two in my explanation.

"Fine," I said, admitting defeat. "First, Max kidnapped Silvio, hid him in the vampire's nest and tied him up with silver chains. Then he kidnapped me, with the help of the police."

"Constable Brown?"

I nodded.

"He must be one of the missing officers."

"He's not missing. He's toast."

"Toast?"

"Dust. He was a vampire," I clarified. "Now, he's a little pile of ashes."

Vincent raised his brows. "You killed him?"

I nodded.

"Tell me, what color ashes did he turn into?"

"Um, red. Like a deep crimson. It was quite a beautiful color, actually."

"Hm." Vincent frowned.

Never a good sign.

"Is it significant?" I asked. "The color of the ashy leftovers, I mean?"

"Well, every vampire bloodline can be identified by a unique color—in their eyes when they're hungry, in their nailbeds, and in their remains. It's useful in helping identify who belongs to whom, and keeping an eye on what types of activities each bloodline is involved in."

"So, who are the crimson ones?"

"They're the nasty ones," Vincent said with a shake of his head. "Really nasty."

"Of course, they are. Why couldn't they be the docile, puppy-loving kind?"

"I don't think there is a docile, puppy-loving kind."

"Wait, did you say police *officers*?" I asked. "As in, more than one is missing?"

"Yes, two. Constable Brown, who it seems isn't so much missing as he is refuse, and another, um…Senior Constable—"

"Gregory Allan," I said, with a heavy heart.

Vincent frowned. "Why is that name so familiar? I feel like —*wait*, he's not the one from the unfortunate hearse incident, is he?"

I nodded. "That's him."

"Is he dust, too?" Vincent asked, and I shook my head.

"No. He wasn't a vampire. He was just a man, but now I'm pretty sure he's dead."

"Did you, you know—?"

"Kill him? No. Michael and Ian, took care of that—"

"*Ian*?"

I chuckled. "I know, right? Not very Nosferatu or Prince of Darkness, is it?"

Vincent shook his head.

"They were the ones who murdered him." I felt sad. SC Allan didn't deserve to die. He had a life. He had friends and family and hobbies and interests... Well, I'm assuming he did. It's not like I'd gotten to know him well, at least not beyond him arresting me.

"And you're sure he's dead?"

I shrugged. "Michael said he took care of him, so..."

Vincent shook his head. "I despise it when innocent people die as a result of paranormal activity. It's been happening for far too long."

"Yet you never get used to it, right?" I asked.

"Indeed, you don't," Vincent agreed. "Anyway, please continue your tale. I find myself needing a distraction."

"Okey dokey, where was I?"

"Max murdered his brother."

"Right. He murdered Dante, then kidnapped his father, then me, and then his sister. He even faked his own kidnapping. I'm telling you, he's cray-cray."

"Wait—"

"I guess, 'was' cray-cray is more appropriate, given he's, you know, dead."

"How did he—"

"How else would you describe a lycan that colluded with vampires to kill off their family, put a Blood Bounty on my head, and then sat there and did nothing when they sold off his brother's werewolf parts to the highest bidder?"

"I need to lie down," Vincent said, easing himself onto the stiff, blue hospital chair at my bedside.

"I had to sit and listen to him rambling on about how stupid birthright is, and how crap humans are...blah, blah, blah. My God could that guy talk. And talk and talk. He just loved the sound of his own voice."

Vincent raised a brow.

"What's that look for, Mr. Smirky McSmirkison?" I asked, but I knew exactly what he was smirking at.

"Nothing." He smiled. "Please continue."

"Where was I?" I asked. "Doesn't matter. You get the picture."

"I do, but what I don't understand is why Max would allow Dante's heart transplanted into your body? He was well aware of the consequences—"

"Oh, he didn't have anything to do with the transplant," I replied. "He was as surprised as all of us."

Vincent's brows shot up and his eyes widened.

"I know, right? Seems the big mystery still needs answering. Anyway," I said, before I got too sidetracked. "I've been thinking, if the Patrons didn't know anything about my transplant, and Max didn't know anything about it, then how the hell did it happen? I mean, we know when the experiments started." I counted off on my fingers. "And we know when they ended. We know about the black-market organ trade, and we know Dante's werewolf heart ended up in me, but we just don't know how. It stands to reason that there's a third player—a serious contender, too—with a lot at stake, and... Why are you looking at me like that?" I asked, suddenly conscious that Vincent was staring.

"It's nothing. It's...well, it's not nothing, actually. It's definitely something."

"That clears things up."

"What I mean to say is, we have a problem."

I raised my brows. "You're only just figuring this out now?"

He stood abruptly. "No, I mean, *you* have a werewolf heart."

"Are you okay?" I reached for his brow so I could check his temperature. "Because we have moved well past the shocked and surprised phase of this adventure."

"Just, shoosh. If what you say is true, you received Dante's heart."

"Didn't I just tell you that?"

"Dante is heir to the De Benedetto pack."

"No, he *was* heir. Now he's dead."

"It's much more complicated than that," Vincent said. "A werewolf's heart is the essence of—"

"Yeah, yeah, I know this story. Max told me," I said, raising my hand. "A werewolf's heart is the very essence of its identity or *raison d'être* or whatever you want to call it. It's what makes them werewolves…yadda, yadda. So, while Dante's heart is still beating, Max couldn't be heir. I told you this before."

"No, you didn't."

"Yeah. I did." Didn't I? "Okay, I may have blah, blah, blahhed over some of it, but that's what I meant, generally speaking."

Vincent pinched the bridge of his nose.

"Headache?" I asked.

He released the grip on his nose and glared at me. Someone was testy.

"Clarissa, you don't seem to be grasping the seriousness of this situation. With Max dead, and you with Dante's heart, you do realize you are now the heir to the De Benedetto pack?"

I snorted. "Yeah, but no. I mean, I guess technically I am, but only technically. But I'm not a werewolf, and I certainly don't want to be heir. I don't want to be alpha, either. I told Max as much. I even promised I wouldn't tell anyone whose heart I had, and that he could do what he wanted with the pack. He seemed okay with that, especially after he tried to frame me for stabbing Silvio and Donatella."

Vincent's brows rose again. "Did you blah, blah, blah over that part, too?"

I shrugged. "Didn't seem relevant, especially seeing Donatella and Silvio aren't dead."

As Vincent was getting his head around the massive amount of information I dumped on him in such a short time, I became conscious of a fine mist forming at the foot of my bed, and watched with fascination as Poppy materialized before my eyes. Seeing her made my heart sing, metaphorically speaking, of course.

"Hey," she said, and Vincent, who'd been unaware of her presence until she spoke, screeched like a cocky at sunrise, and staggered back three steps, sagging back into the chair and clutching his chest.

"*Sonofabitch*!"

It was all I could do not to double over with laughter. "Stealthy, isn't she?" I chuckled.

Vincent stared at me, and then scowled at Poppy.

"Sorry," Poppy mumbled. "But it's urgent."

She looked paler than usual, as hard as that was to imagine, and was fidgeting with the hem of her dress. Whatever she was about to tell me, it knew it wouldn't be good.

"What's wrong?" I asked. "Are you okay?"

"I'm fine, but it's going to get really ugly here in a few minutes," she replied.

That certainly got Vincent's attention. He stood and leaned back into a defensive fighting stance. "What's going on? Are we under attack?"

Paranoid much?

"Not exactly," Poppy said. "But sort of."

"Who is it? Is it werewolves? Vampires? Gargoyles? Did Sonny forget to pay them again?"

"What?" I asked.

"Worse," Poppy said.

"What could be worse than—"

I was about to shoot off a list of things that were potentially worse than werewolves, vampires and gargoyles, starting with Drew warbling out *Jesse's Girl* at Thursday night karaoke (seriously, he couldn't pick a song that was written this century?), when I heard raised voices at the nurses' station just outside my room.

"Oh, no," I groaned.

"What?" Vincent said, springing back to his feet. "What is it?"

"I demand to see Clarissa Hunt!"

"Not again," I said, covering my face with my hands.

"Friend of yours?" Vincent asked, straightening.

"It's our dad," Poppy said. "That's what I was trying to tell you. He's *here*."

"Ohhh. Well, this will be interesting, won't it?" Vincent mused.

The poor bastard had no idea what he was in for.

"I really need to remove him as my emergency contact," I said, scrubbing my face. "I'd be better off changing it to Drew… or you!" I pointed at Vincent.

"Me? I don't think—"

My father burst into the room and passed right *through* Poppy as he rushed to my bedside. Judging by the disgusted expression on her face, and the way she shuddered and dry-retched, I'm going to say it wasn't an experience she wanted to repeat.

"Clarissa, sweetheart, thank God you're alright," Dad said, scooping me up in one of his trademark hugs, and squeezing the air from my lungs. "They told me you were in some kind of construction accident. What the hell happened?"

"Daddy," I squeaked. "Daddy…*air*!" He released me and held me at arm's length.

"Sorry. I'm just… Well, I'm relieved. I got a call to say you were injured. I was on the sixth hole at the time but rushed here as soon as I could."

"After he finished his round, I'll bet," Poppy jibed.

"That freeway is a damned nightmare at this time of day. It took me nearly two hours to get here." Dad stopped to take a breath, and that's when he noticed Vincent standing primly at the foot of the bed. "And who the hell are you?" Dad growled.

"Mr. Hunt," Vincent said, extending his hand in a friendly gesture (he really was getting good at that). "Pleased to meet you. I'm Vincent—"

"Is this your fault?" Dad demanded, ignoring Vincent's polite gesture of greeting, and I'm pretty sure Vincent recoiled slightly. "If it is, I promise you'll be hearing from my lawyer."

"Ohmygod!" Poppy groaned. "There he goes again with the lawyers. How embarrassing."

I rolled my eyes in agreement and sat up properly. "Daddy, calm down," I said. "This is Vincent. He's, um, he's a client. He's just visiting."

Dad gave Vincent a quick once-over and nodded. "Anthony Hunt," he said, taking Vincent's hand, which was still outstretched. "Who's your tailor?"

I had to bite my lip to stop myself from snorting like one of my Aunt Brigit's prized Duroc hogs. Only my father could go from threatening legal action to discussing men's couture in a matter of microseconds.

"No, don't tell me," he continued. "Is it Germanicos?"

Vincent looked like a deer in the headlights, which wasn't an unusual reaction when most people met my father for the first time. It made me think of how well Nash had handled their meeting, and how calm and collected he'd been. Vincent didn't look anywhere near as calm and collected. He looked like he was ready to make a run for it.

Just goes to show, even two-thousand-year-old immortals aren't immune to my father's formidable tirades.

"Or is it Oscar's?"

"Um, no, actually, it's Adriano Carbone," Vincent replied when he finally regained some equilibrium.

Dad snapped his fingers. "Ah! That was my next guess. He's a good man. I buy two or three suits from him every year. So," he said turning his attention back to me. "What happened?"

"It's silly, really," I said. "I was out on a photoshoot at the old sanatorium in Sunbury and it seems they had some demolition work scheduled, only I didn't know. They did some blasting and I got in the way."

"Wow! You're so good at this." Poppy beamed. "Isn't she good at this?"

A wry smile crept across Vincent's lips and he nodded. "Indeed."

"Brilliant," Dad said, clapping and rubbing his hands together. "So, who do I get to sue over this?"

FOURTEEN

TWO BOWLS OF CRAPPY HOSPITAL CUSTARD and a Tetra Pak of apple juice later, the door to my room creaked open, and Sonny peered in.

"Is it safe to enter?" he asked.

"Depends," I replied. "Who's with you?" I was exhausted and hardly in the mood for any more Stooge shenanigans, after barely surviving Daddy's flying visit.

"No one. Just me."

I smiled. "In that case, come on in. I can tell you all about the time Vincent met my father and the two of them spent forty-five minutes arguing about which was better fabric for a morning suit; wool twill or silk blend. It was riveting."

Sonny slid gracefully into the room and shut the door behind him. Good golly, but he was a fine specimen of a man. Nobody, and I do mean NOBODY filled out a pair of 501s the way he did. And don't even get me started on how his arms and chest looked under that black Bonds t-shirt. Yowsers. Just looking at him made my mouth water and my fingertips ache to touch him. I'm not even kidding—they *ached*. Other parts of me were experiencing their own kind of ache, too, but not in a bad way.

"I heard. Sorry I missed it." He smiled just before he planted a wonderfully gentle kiss on my forehead. "Who won?"

"Daddy, of course," I replied. "Vincent's on his way to get counseling."

"I wouldn't worry too much about Vincent. He's a tough cookie."

"You haven't met my dad."

"Not yet. But, I will, and when I do, he's going to love me."

I raised my brows. "That's pretty presumptuous, isn't it?"

"Not really. I can be very charming when I want to be." He dragged the visitors' armchair closer to the side of my bed and laced his fingers with mine. Well, wasn't that just...delightful.

"Actually, I was talking about you meeting my dad. Who says you're ever going to have the pleasure?"

"I think we both know the answer to that," he said, bringing my hand up to his mouth and kissing the back of it.

#allthetingles

"Which brings me to the gigantic bone I have to pick with you, mister," I said, trying to focus while battling the dopamine brain fog that seemed to trigger every time Sonny was around.

"Oh? And what's that?"

I braced myself, because truth be told, I wasn't sure what I hoped the answer to my burning question would be. The only thing I did know was I had to ask it.

"Did you know about the lycan life mate thing before we... we... *You know*?"

"Had sex?" he said, with a quirk of his mouth that revealed the ridiculously cute dimple in his left cheek.

"Yes," I replied, still mortified by how I'd thrown myself at him and seduced him with my frilly, fancy under things and slobbery werewolf kisses.

"You know, if you're old enough to do it, you should be able to say it," Sonny said.

I exhaled. "Fine. Did you know about the lycan life mate thing before we…had sex?"

He pinned me with his glorious green eyes and studied my face. What was there to study? Either he knew or he didn't know. How hard could it be?

"*Well*? Did you?" I pressed.

"Will you get angry if I say yes?"

"Very possibly."

"And if I say no?"

"I'll get angry because that'd be a lie."

A broad smile split his face. "So, you already know the answer, then?"

I nodded. "What I don't understand, though, is if you knew the consequences, why did you, you know, let it happen?"

Sonny threw back his head and laughed. It was wonderfully lyrical and reminded me of pan pipes, but not in a weird, new-agey way. "Let it happen? *Let it*? We've already talked about this, Clarissa. I couldn't have stopped it, even if I was insane enough to want to."

"Quit it," I said, giving him a good-natured swat. "I'm serious."

"So am I," he replied. "You can be very persuasive."

"Oh, come on," I whined. "Tell meeee."

"Well, if I'm being honest, I wasn't entirely sure the life mate thing would apply to us. I mean, you're not technically a were-wolf, and I'm… I'm…"

I shivered in anticipation. Was he going to tell me what he was? Finally?

"I'm something else entirely," he said.

Urgh. I was never going to find out what he was, was I?

"But that first time we kissed, I absolutely knew."

"You knew what?"

His cheeks flushed. "Oh, come on. You're not going to make me say it, are you?"

"Ah, yeah. I think I am."

"Fine," he grumbled. "If you insist. Before we...you know."

"If you're old enough to do it, you're old enough to say it."

"You want to hear this or not?" he said, his face all serious and mock-peeved.

I nodded. "Sorry."

"Alright, so before we had sex, I already knew how amazing you were."

I scoffed and Sonny frowned.

"You disagree?" he asked.

"Ah, yeah. I mean, amazing? *Me*? Pfft."

"Don't do that," he said.

"Do what?"

"Don't put yourself down like that."

"Oh, come on, Sonny. Let's be real. I'm a train wreck."

He stiffened and a serious expression clouded his face. "I disagree."

"Oh, please. You know firsthand that I'm a walking disaster. I keep getting killed, over and over again. I run off at the mouth incessantly. I destroy perfectly good property. I can't balance a check book for nuts. I hurt my dead sister's feelings—"

"You hurt Poppy's feelings?"

I nodded. "My cat likes everyone on the planet better than she likes me, and I eat far too much ice cream."

"And none of that matters to me. What matters is what's in here." He tapped the center of my breastbone.

"My werewolf heart, you mean?"

"In a way." He pinned me with his emerald gaze. "It's who you are *despite* your werewolf heart."

I swallowed hard. "Oh?"

"That's how I knew," Sonny said, his voice soft, the caress of his fingertips gentle on the back of my hand.

"Knew what?" I squeaked.

"That you truly are the best kind of person. Here you are with a werewolf heart beating in your chest, and believe me when I tell you they are one of the most vicious predators I've ever encountered, but not you. You're still the smartest, funniest," he paused. "Best woman I've ever known."

"Um, okay. Thank you?" I said as heat rushed through my body.

"A different person, a lesser person, would have gone completely insane by now, not to mention become so vicious there'd be no controlling them. Not you, though." He brushed an errant hair from my face. "You're just…you."

"And let's face it, I'm pretty irresistible."

"You are as far as I'm concerned."

Was he blushing?

"And Vincent. He loves me, you know?" I said with a smile.

"Does he now?"

I nodded. "Told me so himself. We're like besties now."

"Really?"

"Yep. Jealous?"

"Hardly."

"Why not?"

"Well, since I'm pretty sure this," he waggled a finger in front of my face, "is just one of your infamous Clarissa moments when you make up stories to deflect…"

I shot him my best stink-eye.

"Er…you know what? Never mind. I'm sure he does love you. It's not that hard to believe."

I felt my cheeks flush. What was he saying? What was he doing? What—

"So, what if you're a little quirky, and God knows you talk far too much, but…" Sonny sighed and dropped his gaze momentarily before locking eyes with me. "Still, I think you're amazing."

Be still, my beating werewolf heart.

How could such a simple, gentle gesture make me feel so damn gooey inside? *How?*

"So, what I'm saying," Sonny said, fidgeting with his fingernails or cuticles or something. It was interesting to watch. "What I'm saying is, maybe we could, you know, give this life mate thing a chance." He dropped his eyes. "If you want to, that is. Or not. I mean whatever. I was just being stupid. Big misunderstanding. Forget about it."

Sonny looked at me through those thick lashes of his and I couldn't help but smile. He was so adorable when he was flustered; his cheeks got all rosy and his eyes became greener, if you could even imagine that. Just, adorable

"Will you say something, *please*?" Sonny whined. "Normally, I can't get you to shut up for more than two minutes at a time, but now you decide to say nothing? Speak, woman."

"Well," I said, choosing my words carefully. "I think, maybe…"

"Oh, come *oooooonnn*!" Sonny pleaded. "Just put me out of my misery! Are you in or are you out?"

I laughed, which resulted in Sonny looking crestfallen. I had to put him out of his misery. "I'm in, Sonny. I'm definitely in."

His eyes snapped to mine, and a smile split his face. Whooping like a cowboy, Sonny pulled me onto his lap and into his tight embrace.

"Careful! You're going to tangle my IV lines," I squealed.

But Sonny wasn't listening. He was too busy nuzzling my neck and gently nipping the tender spot under my jaw.

Holy mother of wow!

"When you're well again," he murmured, as he planted soft, wet kisses across my collar bone. "I've got plans for you, young lady. Very important, very urgent plans."

My head lolled back, and I reveled in the warm, fuzzy feeling that was simmering low in my belly.

"Aha," I said, unable to form any coherent thoughts. "Plans. Yes. I like plans."

I was just settling into what was shaping up to be an extremely pleasant afternoon of tingles and flutters, when the sounds of country music snapped me back to my senses.

I pulled back and looked at Sonny, who was fumbling with his phone. *"Take Me Home, Country Roads."* I said, "John Denver? Really?"

Sonny mouthed, *sorry*, and answered the call, an apologetic look on his face.

After his curt, *hello*, he didn't speak, just worked his jaw as whomever was on the other end of the line rambled on. I couldn't hear who it was, or what they were saying, but they were really pissing Sonny off because he suddenly reeked of rotting fruit and rubbing alcohol.

Yuck.

I wriggled off his lap and back onto the hospital bed, just as Sonny punched the end button on his phone, shoved it back into his pocket, and swore under his breath.

"Something wrong?" I asked, noting his creased brow and thinned lips. "You look a little off."

"No. Nothing's wrong."

"Well, it doesn't seem like it was nothing. Who was that?"

"No one."

"So, no one called you about nothing and now you're all—" I waved my hand at him. "This."

Sonny stood and stalked to the end of the bed. "I have to go."

"Go? Go where?"

Panic. Rising.

"Away. I have…" Raking his hand through his hair. "I have some business to attend to."

"What kind of business?"

"Important business. Important, personal—"

"Does this have anything to do with the life mate thing? Because if you're having second thoughts—"

"No. It's nothing to do with that," he said, walking back to my side and taking my hand. "And no, I don't have cold feet. It's the opposite, I can't wait to start this adventure with you."

"Why do I feel like there's a but coming?"

"Because there's a but coming," he replied.

"You have to go," I said, my heart sinking. I didn't know what was wrong, but there was definitely something afoot. I knew it just like I knew the werewolves were going to attack me and Nash at the Myer Clinic.

#premonitionalert

"Yeah. I have to go."

"When?"

"Now."

"Now? Are you kidding?"

"I wish I was."

"How long will you be gone?"

He shook his head. "I don't know. A day, maybe two. I'll make it as short as possible."

"Will you call me while you're gone?"

I heard a high-pitched beeping that was getting faster and faster, and recognized it as the heart monitor I was hooked up to. Clearly I was getting quite agitated.

"No. I won't be able to call."

"Why not?" I snapped. "Sonny, you're freaking me out."

He kissed my hand and squeezed it reassuringly. "Don't freak out. It's nothing. I just… I…"

"Have to go. I know. So, go."

"Don't be mad," he said. "Please."

"I'm not mad. I'm fine. I'm confused, but it's okay. I just figure the sooner you go, the sooner you can do what you have to do, and the sooner you can come back, and we can get this party started."

"I'm really sorry," he said. "But I promise, everything will be okay. Nothing will happen to you while I'm gone."

"Of course, it won't." I smiled, hoping it looked more convincing than it felt. "My new bestie Vincent will look after me."

Then Sonny smiled at me, and I changed my mind. I didn't hope my smile looked more convincing than it felt. I hoped it looked more convincing than Sonny's.

FIFTEEN

FOUR DAYS AND I HADN'T HEARD SO MUCH AS A PEEP FROM SONNY, so when I got the message that Vincent wanted to see me, I dropped what I was doing (changing Miss Miranda's kitty litter; she'd just have to hang on until I got back home to finish the job) and scrambled to the cathedral as quickly as I could.

Of course, when I arrived, Poppy in tow, and there was no sign of Sonny, I deflated like last Saturday night's birthday party balloon garland.

"Lovely to see you again, Poppy." Vincent smiled as he showed us into his office. "And you, Clarissa. How—"

"Quit with the small talk, Vincent," I barked. "Where's Sonny?" I skulked past him and headed straight for his liquor trolley.

"She's in a pleasant mood," he said to Poppy.

"You have no idea,"

"Did you hear me?" I filled a crystal glass with two generous shots of whiskey and glared at Vincent. "I asked, where's Sonny?"

"He's away, on assignment. I thought you knew this. He assured me he'd informed you before he left."

"He did," Poppy chimed. "She's just not happy about it."

"I thought *I* was his assignment," I pressed, ignoring Poppy and her special comments.

Vincent's brows shot up. "You're not his only assignment, Clarissa. Surely you realized this?"

I sculled the whiskey and slammed the glass back on the tray. "Clearly I hadn't."

I felt foolish.

I felt like crying.

I felt enraged.

I felt completely lost.

"Clarissa, are you alright?" Vincent asked. "You don't quite seem yourself."

"She's freaking out over Sonny," Poppy replied. "He hasn't called since he left."

"Oh," Vincent replied. "I can see how that would be distressing. He's perfectly safe, though, if that's what you're worried about. He's in no danger whatsoever."

"Then tell me where he is," I said.

"I can't," he replied.

"Can't or won't?"

"Does it matter? I can't say anything, so I won't. It's not my story to tell."

I rolled my eyes. "You and your protocols. Seriously. How can I even be sure he'll ever come back and tell me himself?"

"He'll be back, and he'll tell you everything. Trust me."

I snorted. "You're kidding right?"

Vincent crossed his arms and cocked his head. "I thought we'd moved beyond the mistrust and sarcasm stage of our relationship, Clarissa?"

"You have," Poppy said. "She's just being extra difficult. If you ask me, she's just sex starved."

"*Poppy*!" I shrieked. "Oh my God. When are you ever going to learn to shut up and stop blurting out inappropriate statements like that?"

"Probably never." She grinned.

"Annoying, isn't it?" Vincent asked, turning to me. I just sneered at him and sat down in my usual chair. It was clear he wasn't going to give up any information about where Sonny was, who he was with, or when he'd be back. I was just going to have to be patient and wait it out. Couldn't wait to see how *that* turned out.

"So," I said, trying to act less like a little bitch and more like a grown up. "If you didn't call me here to talk about Sonny, what did you call me for?"

"Well," Vincent said, motioning for Poppy to sit on the couch, as he took his place on the throne. "I've been thinking."

I let my head loll back against the headrest of the chair I'd claimed as my own and groaned. "That's never good."

Vincent glared at me. "There will be none of that, Clarissa."

"What? I'm not lying. The last time you had a bright idea, I ended up with a silver dagger in my chest. Remember?"

"You hardly let me forget," he replied.

"It's all she ever talks about," Poppy added. "That and Sonny. 'I miss Sonny. Why hasn't he called? Sonny. Sonny. Sonny.'"

"Sounds exhausting," Vincent replied.

"You don't know the half of it."

"If you two don't mind," I interjected before it turned into a full-blown, *let's bitch about Clarissa* session. "Vincent has an idea he'd like to share with me, so why don't we let him?"

Vincent nodded. "Thank you," he said to me before turning to Poppy. "We'll talk later."

FFS. I knew introducing the two of them would be a jumbo-sized mistake. I was such an idiot. I mentally kicked myself.

"So, are you going to share this marvelous idea with me or are you going to force me to guess? Because I'm getting pretty good at the whole mind-reading thing."

"Guessing won't be necessary," Vincent said. "I'd like to offer you a job."

That sure got my attention.

"But I have a job," I replied, peering at him. "I have a very good job."

"Yes, but this job is better. This job is working for me."

I snort-laughed and gave him a couple of little golf claps. "Good one, Vincent," I said. "Very funny, but I hate to tell you, it's not April Fool's."

"I'm well aware of that."

"Then what's with the joke?" I asked, still chuckling.

Poppy leaned over and nudged me. "Read the room, Rissy. I don't think he's joking."

My head snapped back to Vincent and I noted the lack of mirth in his expression. "Oh, wow. You're serious?" I asked. "Sorry. I just thought, you know, jokes—why would you offer me a job?"

"Because, much as it pains me to admit, I need you, Clarissa. It seems I've spent far too long underestimating humans and how much they actually know about us."

"Us?"

"The Patrons, the Inner World, all the paranormal activity that exists around them. People know far more than I ever gave them credit for." He sighed. "I was a fool. I had no idea so much information was out there, all over the interwebs. There's a whole new world out there I know nothing about, and as you've made abundantly clear on several occasions that has to change; for my own good."

"And?" I pressed, thoroughly enjoying the awkward conversation and Vincent's embarrassing admissions. This whole situation, asking for help, acknowledging that he'd been wrong all along, and confessing he needed my expertise, must have been KILLING him.

"And…" Vincent shifted in his seat and clenched his jaw. "I need your help. It's obvious the interwebs is a very important tool that could help us perform our duties far more efficiently."

"Why does he keep calling it the interwebs?" Poppy whispered.

I shushed her. "Quiet. I don't want to miss a word of this."

"So, after some thought and deliberations with my counterparts in the other three regions, it seems logical to invite Clarissa to join us, the Patrons that is, so together we are not only better equipped to keep the balance between the Inner and Outer worlds, but so we could also continue to investigate the mystery of how Clarissa ended up with Dante's heart."

God, I loved it when Vincent was all nervous and twitchy and totally unsure of himself. Not only was it a rare occurrence, but his stream-of-consciousness babbling was utterly delightful. It was a joy to behold.

"What mystery?" Poppy asked. "Max did it, now he's dead. No more problem… Or am I missing something?"

"Max was only part of the puzzle," Vincent explained. "Yes, he hired the vampire scum to kill Dante, and as a result, they sold his organs on the black market, but the real mystery is, who bought the organs from Max? How did someone get their hands on the files from our hybrid development program and successfully restart it? Why was Clarissa chosen to be an organ recipient, and why was her surgery so successful when others had been such monumental failures? And maybe, most importantly, who's funding all the surgeries, and to what end? Because, I can pretty much guarantee there are more hybrids like your sister out there, Poppy, and I'd bet my bottom dollar the others have been nowhere near as successful as Clarissa."

Poppy looked from Vincent to me then back to Vincent again. "He makes a compelling argument, doesn't he?"

"I guess so," I said, not wanting to give too much away.

"Thank you," Vincent added.

"How long do I have to think about it?" I asked.

"Between now and when you leave here today."

"How many hours a week do I need to work?"

"That's up to you."

"And the salary?"

"Also, up to you."

Niiiiice. The deal was sounding better and all the time.

"Do I get my own office?"

"No," he said.

"Do I get an assistant?"

"If you need one."

"Can I call you Vinnie?"

"Absolutely not."

"What if I only do it when we're alone?"

"Clarissa!" he barked. "You're playing on my very last nerve."

"Fine," I said. "You don't have to get all uncool and heavy on me."

Poppy frowned at me. "Uncool and heavy?"

I shrugged. "I don't know. I heard it on TV once."

"I do wish you'd concentrate, Clarissa," Vincent snapped. "This is the job of a lifetime, and you're over there taking pot-shots at it? I'm giving you the opportunity to set up the online presence for the Patrons from scratch. You can do whatever the hell you like with it, the whole thing! You get to monitor the dark web for any unusual, or covert, Inner World activity, and you get to do this and receive an extremely generous wage offering for your troubles." He sighed heavily. "What's there to even think about?"

"Wow, that was quite an admission, Vincent," Poppy said. "Did that hurt as much as it looked like it did?"

"You have no idea," Vincent replied, scrubbing his hands down his face.

I beamed at Vincent. This had to be one of the best days in the history of ever. "And in return, you promise to help me investigate the mystery of my werewolf heart and who is responsible for the whole fiasco?"

Vincent nodded. "I'll make it my very highest priority." He held up his hand, thumb and pinkie fingers outstretched, and gave it a little shake. "Scout's honor."

I didn't have the heart to tell him he'd just given me the *shaka sign*. He was trying so hard.

SIXTEEN

THE MOMENT I OPENED MY FRONT DOOR, I knew something was wrong. I was slowly coming to terms with my growing lycan instincts; those spidey-senses that tingled intermittently, alerting me to potential danger, or human emotion, or the presence of processed meats when I was feeling peckish (which, as it happens, was becoming an increasingly frequent occurrence).

This wasn't a processed meat situation, though.

This was something very different.

There was no sign of Poppy for one, and she never missed an opportunity to make her presence felt. That kid was all up in my grill 24/7/365, so her lack of hovering and yammering was a bit disconcerting. Miss Miranda wasn't anywhere to be seen either. If I wasn't accosted by Poppy the moment I walked in the door, Miss Miranda was usually there, meowing her floofy, black butt off, demanding food, or pats, or a litter clean.

But today, they were both conspicuously absent… But that didn't mean no one was home.

I didn't actually need to see him to know Sonny was there. I could smell him the moment I'd walked in the door. Normally, his tantalizing aroma of juicy peaches and woodsy pheromones was a very pleasant experience. Not today, though. Today there was something else lingering in the air; something that smelled like sour milk and month-old Stilton.

Yyyyyyuck.

"Sonny?" I called out, putting my bag down and slipping out of my boots and into my new slippers. I knew it was a *closing the gate after the horse had bolted* situation, but I was not going to be caught barefoot and stranded on a kitchen mat surrounded by a sea of shattered glass ever again.

Plus, I just don't think I could take another lecture from Mum.

I was relieved when he answered, and headed straight into the kitchen, where I had plans to, a) lecture him for not contacting me for over a week, and b) kissing him within an inch of his life. I was angry, but a girl has needs.

When I swung the kitchen door open, Sonny was sitting at the dining table, looking better than any man had the right to in his well-worn biker jacket, white t-shirt and three-day growth. He was breathtaking and the mere sight of him was enough to make my mouth water.

I took a few rushed steps, eager to greet him. He stood from his chair, however, putting down the coffee mug he'd been holding, but didn't move toward me. That's when I noticed we weren't alone.

There was no mistaking the resemblance between Sonny and the burly man-mountain standing behind him. He was about Sonny's weight and height, and the shape of their faces, the cut of their chiseled jaws, the emerald shimmer of their eyes, all same…same…and, same. But for the color of their hair, the tall, dark stranger was the spitting image of Sonny. They could very well have been twins. Maybe they *were* twins? Sonny hadn't mentioned being a twin, though… Had he? He hadn't mentioned having any siblings at all.

A sudden wave of nausea washed over me. I felt icky. My tummy knotted and I broke out into a sweat; not a getting-pulled-over-by-the-police kind of sweat, that would have been beyond embarrassing, but a sweat nonetheless.

Having both mammoth men in such close proximity could have been causing the nausea and claustrophobia, but I think what was putting me on edge was not knowing who the new guy was, or if he was the bearer of good or bad tidings.

"Is this her?" the stranger asked as he eyed me from across the room. "Is this the mongrel you want to abandon your lineage for?"

I'm going to go out on a limb and say bad tidings.

I bristled and could feel my werewolf heart push adrenaline through my body like a freight train. "Who are you calling a mongrel?" I growled, planting my hands on my hips and staring him down. "And what lineage are we talking about, exactly?"

The stranger threw me a lopsided grin that was eerily similar to the one Sonny used when he was trying to charm me, but Strange Sonny Doppelganger wasn't about to get any special treatment from me until he answered a few questions and had a sharp change in attitude. And if he wasn't prepared to play nice, he was going to get a stern talking to and possibly a nasty Chinese Burn.

"Apologies, do you prefer half-breed?" he continued. "Freak of nature? How about—"

"Enough!" Sonny said, slamming his hands on the table and leaning forward. "You will not speak to her that way."

Much to my surprise, Doppelganger Sonny backed down with no further fuss.

Hmmm.

He was surprisingly obedient for such a boorish bloke.

"What's going on?" I asked Sonny. "Where the hell have you been, and who is this giant douche canoe?"

Sonny scowled at me. "Clarissa, name calling isn't going to help the situation," he scolded. "No matter how true it is."

He was right, of course, but I just didn't care.

"He started it," I said.

"Oh, please," Doppelganger Sonny whined.

"What part of 'that's enough' did the two of you misunderstand?" Sonny really sounded annoyed, so I mumbled an apology, not that I meant it.

Sonny nodded in approval. "Now, Clarissa, this is my brother."

"You have a *brother*?" I gaped.

"He has three brothers," Doppelganger Sonny nodded. "And two sisters."

I narrowed my eyes at Sonny. "I had no idea…"

I was a bundle of mixed emotions—sad, ashamed, embarrassed, confused. How could I not know any of this? I'd always prided myself on being such a good listener. I always made sure I paid attention when someone was speaking and to remember the details—

"Isn't that right?"

I could feel two intense pairs of green eyes focus on me "Um, I beg your pardon?" Okay, so perhaps I wasn't such a good listener, after all.

"I was just saying it's shameful that Sunshine hadn't at least mentioned me, or any of our siblings to you," Doppelganger Sonny said. "I thought surely if you were as important as he'd led me to believe, he'd have told you about us. Makes you wonder, doesn't it… Um, I'm sorry, I've forgotten. What's your name again?" He leaned into me. "It's hard to keep track sometimes."

"Clarissa," Sonny and I both chorused, and Sonny shot me an apologetic look. He needn't have bothered. I wasn't perturbed by his brother's obvious, and PS: childish, attempt to rattle me. Neither Sonny nor I had been angels in the past, not literally, I don't think. I'd been with my fair share of weirdos and, if the Inner World gossip were to be believed, Sonny had apparently bedded half the females in both the paranormal and human worlds. So, if Old Mate was hoping to get a rise out of me, he'd one hundred percent failed.

I was, however, bothered by the fact that I knew so little about Sonny. I didn't know about his family or his species or his favorite song. Heck, I didn't even know his full name —*wait*.

"Hold it," I said, and I felt my mouth inadvertently pop open. "Why did you call him Sunshine?"

"Excuse me?" Doppelganger Sonny said.

"Before, when you were babbling on about whatever it was, you called Sonny Sunshine. Why?"

"Because that's his name," Doppelganger Sonny said. "Sunshine River, Prince of Keijujen Valtakunta."

"That's enough," Sonny said.

"Collagen Valcunt—*what*?"

"The Realm of the Fae," Doppelganger Sonny said in such a way that only ending the sentence with *dumbass* could have made me feel any more inadequate.

I looked at Sonny. "Your name is *Sunshine*? And you're a *prince*?"

"A faerie prince," Sonny's brother chimed in.

Sonny nodded.

I had so many thoughts coursing through my mind, not least of which was the fact that Sonny's real name was *SUNSHINE* (PS: what kind of asshats would call their kid Sunshine, by the way?) and that he was, of all things, a faerie. I mean, I'd guessed everything from wizard to hobbit and most things in between, but faerie? Seriously?

"This is too much," I said, rubbing my eyes. "A *faerie*?"

"A faerie *prince*," Doppelganger Sonny said. "She seems to be having trouble digesting that detail."

"And you are?" I interrupted before he cast further aspersions on my intellect.

"Dusty," Sonny said. "Second heir to—"

"Dusty?" I smirked "What kind of weird-ass name—"

"My name is Moondust. Moondust Glow."

"My condolences," I sniped.

"Sunshine here prefers to use more humanized-monikers over our honorable and, might I say, revered, birth names. Apparently, they aren't manly enough for your sad little world." Dusty made air quotes around *manly*, which just made him look like a total wanker.

"Can't say I blame him," I said, eying Sonny and noting the pained look on his face.

"*Pfft*." Dusty waved me off like I was a bothersome fly. "If a man's worth is measured solely by how masculine his name is perceived to be, then there's not much that can be said about the human race, now, is there?" Dusty scoffed.

Hmmm. Old Moondust had a point.

But point or not, he was still being a dick.

"So," I said, clapping my hands together and hoping to change the subject. "Is there a particular reason for this delightful family reunion, or did you just pop by to insult me and drink my coffee?"

Dusty took a big slug from his cup, French vanilla by the smell of it, and grinned. "If it was up to me, neither of us would be here, but Sunshine insisted he needed to speak to you before he left—"

"Left? Left for what?"

"Home, of course. Our father, the king, is abdicating. The time has come."

"The time has come for *what*?"

"For the Phya," he said, clapping Sonny on the back.

"Okay, you just need to stop, and *you* need to start speaking." I glared at Sonny. "What is he talking about? What's a Phya?" I was more confused than I'd ever been, and given all the weird shit I'd encountered in the last month, that was saying something.

"It's the Sacred Ritual of Ascension."

I blinked at Dusty and then back at Sonny, not quite understanding. I mean, I could hear the words, and knew what they meant, but still somehow none of it was computing.

"What does that even mean, ascension?"

"It means to rise. As in, it's time for Sunshine to take his rightful place as King of the Faerie Kingdom and lead our people to further greatness and prosperity."

Dusty was an A-grade jackass. A pompous, liar, liar, pants on fire creep. Not to mention, he was just a big meanie. No way was Sonny the future faerie king. If he was, he'd have told me, right? It's not like that's the kind of detail you forget to mention, to say, your *life mate*.

And yet, when I looked into Sonny's eyes, I knew what Dusty was saying was one hundred percent true. Sonny just hadn't told me any of it.

"You never mentioned anything about being a king." I swung around and glared at Sonny.

"Technically, I'm a prince."

Dusty roared with laughter. "You haven't told her? Oh, brother, is that any way to start a relationship with, well, whatever she is to you? By not telling her the truth? By deceiving her? Tsk tsk, Sunshine. Tsk tsk."

I had to hand it to Dusty. He had a way of distilling the most complex concepts into their most basic principles. *Tsk tsk, Sunshine,* indeed.

"Yes, shame on you," I said, turning to Sonny and scowling at him. "But, there's no time like the present to set things straight, is there? So, why don't you start at *Once upon a time,* and keep going until you reach, *And, they lived happily ever after* and explain to me what Big Bro over here is talking about."

"Little bro," Dusty said, leaning back against my breakfast bar again and crossing his legs at the ankles. It was a move I'd seen Sonny do dozens of times before, and it was kind of sexy on both of them. "Sunshine is the eldest."

"Of course, he is."

The feeling of shame intensified as I truly realized just how little I knew about the man I was so obviously falling for. He knew everything about me, more than any sane person would want to know, and yet up until that moment, I hadn't known anything about him, or even thought to ask.

I was a shit person.

A shit, shit, selfish, narcissistic, shit person.

"So, there are six of you?" I asked. This lack of sharing was going to stop. Immediately. "Siblings, that is."

Dusty rolled his eyes, the smarmy bastard. If he didn't watch his step, he was getting a punch in the onions, tout suite.

"Yes. I have five siblings," Sonny said, reading my expression and realizing his little brother had lit my fuse.

My ability to hold my temper, and my tongue, was not what it used to be, which, if I was being completely honest, wasn't all that good to begin with. Add a hyperactive werewolf heart and ye olde faerie family secrets to the mix, and I had all but lost what little patience I had in the first place.

"After me, there's Dusty, then Bram, Woody, our sister, June and —"

"Juniper Breeze," Dusty snapped. "BramBLE THORN, DriftWOOD Float. Call us by our proper names."

Sonny glared at him. "I will call you whatever I damn well please, Dusty. You'll do well to remember who I am."

"Do *you* remember who you are?" Dusty countered.

"What's that supposed to mean?"

"Have you looked in the mirror lately, brother? You are a

shadow of your former self. You have clearly spent too much time cavorting with these lesser creatures, changing your name, working for the Patrons, living as a human, denying your heritage. Why are you even trying to make yourself into something you're not? You're a warrior. You're a king, for heaven's sake. All this…this..." Dusty waved his hands around. "Fake mortality is simply beneath you."

I could practically see the steam billowing from Sonny's ears.

"I wish you'd just stop it. Stop denigrating yourself by pretending to be one of them, because you're not," Dusty said.

Sonny ignored him, keeping his eyes locked on me.

"Why is this the first I'm hearing any of this?" I asked, hoping it actually was the first time. Because I would have been absolutely devastated if he *had* told me before and I'd just forgotten. I had been a little self-absorbed; wrapped up in my own stuff which, in my defense, had been a lot, but was that even an excuse to know absolutely nothing about Sonny?

Just to reiterate, I'm a shit, shit person.

Dusty pushed himself off the kitchen bench and clapped once. "This, dear woman," he said without so much as a hint of sincerity in his voice. "Is Prince Sunshine River Elämää. First-born son of King Arvo and Queen Helmi, heir to the throne of Keijujen Valtakunta, the faerie realm. He is respected, exalted, a Fae of great honor and wisdom. Trained in over a dozen forms of combat; he has nurtured diplomatic relationships with hundreds, if not thousands, of species, speaks dozens of languages, human and otherwise, has strength and agility the likes of which you will never see again. He has been groomed to be King of the Fae since the day he was born." Dusty was practically beaming. "And you, correct me if I'm wrong, play on the internet for a living, and have a propensity for getting killed. Have I got that right?"

"Why do you have to be such a giant cretin all the time, Dusty?" Sonny asked. "Seriously."

"I'm just being truthful, brother. Something you seem to have forgotten how to do," Dusty said.

I turned to Sonny and frowned. "Is this true?" I asked. It was my turn to cross my arms defensively. "And you better come clean, mister, because I'm running out of patience."

Sonny exhaled deeply and visibly sagged. I wanted to reach out and comfort him; to throw my arms around him and let him know everything would be okay. That it didn't matter if he hadn't told me every single detail about his past, or anything at all, for that matter. I wasn't about to tell him about that time with the nightclub manager and his pet python, so I totally understood the need to keep some things private. Of course, another part of me wanted to kick him in the shin and send him packing for being a duplicitous schmuck. I just wasn't sure which part was going to win out.

"I'll tell you everything," he said, reaching out, resting his hands on my upper arms and drawing me close to him. "No more secrets, okay?"

"Oh, *barf*," Dusty said.

"Do you mind?" I shot him some sneaky stink eye.

"A little. This mushy stuff is a bit *blech*."

"Then maybe you'd like to give us some privacy?" Sonny said.

"My pleasure," Dusty replied, taking three long strides into the living room. "How's this?"

"A little more, please. Somewhere that's not *here*."

Dusty rolled his eyes. "Fine, just don't take too long," he said, tapping his wrist. "Time's a ticking."

Dark-green smoke that smelled like apple pie and butter-scotch filled the room and in the blink of an eye, Dusty was gone.

"Neat trick." I coughed, swatting away the smoke. "Can't say

I'm a big fan of the smoke, though. Makes me wheezy. But that's the least of our problems at the moment, isn't it, Your *Highness*?"

"I was going to tell you, I swear," Sonny said. There was an edge of desperation in his voice I'd never heard before.

Interesting.

"When exactly?" I asked, folding my arms across my chest.

"I wanted to tell you every time I saw you, but I never found the right moment... Or the right words."

"It's really not that hard, Sonny. Here, pay attention." I cleared my throat. "*Hey babe, how was your day? I was thinking maybe sushi for dinner tonight, what do you think? Oh, by the way, I'm a faerie prince and one day I'm going to be summoned back to the palace so I can take my rightful place as the exalted leader of my peeps. Fancy a California Roll?*" I was yelling, submitting to the lycan adrenaline pumping through my veins and I didn't even care. "See, not that hard, *SUN-SHINE*!"

"Look, I know I've upset you—"

"Do you? *DO YOU?* Because I don't think you do. If you did, you would have shown me some respect and told me this major piece of backstory, *FOREVER* ago, and not waited for your really pleasant brother to pop in and blindside me. He's a real charmer, by the way. Your folks must be so proud."

"In my defense, we have had a lot of other stuff going on," he said. "And it's not like you were interrogating me about my family tree."

"So, this is my fault?"

"I never said that."

"Well, it sure seems like that's what you were saying."

Sonny exhaled deeply. "Can we start again, please?"

"I don't know, can we?" I glared at him.

"Truth is, I didn't know how to tell you. It's not that easy. This is a reality I've been running from for three hundred years."

"But why have you been running? What's there to be afraid of—wait, *three hundred years*? How old *are* you?"

"You don't know what it's like," he said, rubbing his hands down his face and ignoring my age question completely. "Having to carry the weight of your family's expectations on your shoulders. It's paralyzing."

"Really? You think I don't know what living up to family pressure is like? You've met my parents, right? No pressure there."

"With all due respect, your situation and mine aren't quite the same. Your parents coddled you and wrapped you in cotton wool."

"Coddled me?"

"Yes, coddled. Your parents lavished you with love and affection and anything your little heart desired."

"Because my *sister died*, and they felt *guilty*!"

"And mine taught me how to load a crossbow before I could even walk."

"So, this is a pissing competition now?"

"No. Of course not. This is coming out all wrong. All I'm trying to say is sometimes it's not about you."

"Well, it's certainly not about you because as it turns out, I have no idea who *you* are. I might have been coddled, but unlike you, at least I've always told you the truth."

"And I can just imagine how that would have gone over. *Hey, Clarissa, yes, I love you and want to be with you and make plans for the future with you, but just keep in mind my family could come for me at any moment and drag my ass back to Keijujen Valtakunta.*"

Uhhmm, did he just say he loved me? *I love you and want to be with you.* I replayed his words in my head. Holy—

"*Where I am destined to rule for one thousand years or more,*" he continued. "*Oh, and there's nothing I can do about it, either. Once I'm called back, I have to go. That was part of the deal*. I'm pretty sure that conversation would have ended with you kicking my ass."

It felt like I'd been slugged in the guts with a wrecking ball as my heart both sang and broke, simultaneously.

"What deal?" I asked, not really knowing what else to say.

"When I was younger." He released a heavy sigh. "Much, much younger, I was a bit of a rebel."

"Shocking," I said.

He smiled at me gently and my heart broke just a little more.

"I didn't want to be a prince, much less be groomed to be king. I wanted to be myself, be…" He took my hand and held it to his chest. "I wanted to be Sonny, to explore and learn and, most of all, be free of the burden of my lineage. My father eventually agreed to let me leave the faerie realm, but on one condition."

I was pretty sure I knew what was coming next but wanted to let Sonny tell me the whole truth.

"I made a sacred *vala*, a promise to my father and the neuvosto; his Council. They would permit me to go anywhere I wanted, do anything I desired, be whatever I chose to be."

"Kind of like Rumspringa?" I asked, trying to make sense of it all.

"Sort of, but with the proviso that, when summoned, I had to return home immediately. No questions. No renegotiation. Just home. Or risk being detained and brought back to the faerie realm in shackles and dishonoring my family."

"Harsh," I said.

"Perhaps, but it was the only way I could get them to agree to let me go." He shook his head, as if in disbelief. "It seemed like such a good deal at the time. I never thought… I never imagined I'd meet anyone like you. That I'd fall so hard and never want to return to my ancestral home. But I did, and now my heart is breaking because I have to go and…and…" He sighed. "And there's nothing I can do about it."

"Surely there must be something we can do," I said, acutely aware that my voice had gone up at least two octaves. "I mean, just don't go. Stay here with me and let Dusty take your place."

"It doesn't work that way, Clarissa. You can't just hand over your lineage," he said. "Peace in the faerie realm is precarious at best. If I don't go back, then another neuvosto can, and will, overthrow my father, and take control of everything, our wealth, our land, the entire realm. They'll strip us of everything, including our magicks. It's happened before. Entire lineages were slaughtered. Our former queen, Apolonia, was murdered, and each of her followers disappeared, presumed murdered, too."

"Oh."

"The other neuvostos, they aren't good people. They're cruel; power-hungry and utterly ruthless. Should any one of them succeed in gaining power, thousands upon thousands of my subjects will die horrible deaths, or be forced to live in abject poverty, slavery, or worse, be banished. Everyone I've ever known and loved would be in grave danger." He shook his head. "I can't be responsible for that. It took centuries for my family to overthrow the tyrants that preceded us, to make our people safe and our realm prosperous once again. If I don't go back, all will be lost and everything we've done will have been for nothing."

"So, that's it? You're just leaving me?"

"No, I'm not leaving you. I could never leave you."

"But you're going away. You're not going to be here. That sounds very much like leaving to me."

"You don't understand. There's no choice for me. This is my destiny. It's also not a responsibility I take lightly. It's my duty."

"All this," I said, twirling my finger in front of his face, "still sounds like a whole lotta leaving, Sonny. Call it what you like, the upshot is you're going away, and I'll be here…all alone." I became aware then of the hot, fat tears streaming down my face.

Great.

My mascara was going to be *everywhere* and Sonny's last

memories of me were going to involve snot and gloopy panda eyes.

"You won't be alone. You have Vincent and Azrael, and your sister." He smiled.

"They're all crazy."

"That they are, but they love you, so I know you'll be safe and happy."

"But none of them is you," I sniffed.

"I know," Sonny said. "But, I can't just turn my back on my people, no matter how much it hurts."

"But, what about me?" I said, choking on the blind panic rising in my throat. "You promised you'd always be with me, to protect me, and—"

"You don't need protecting, Clarissa. You've told me as much a dozen times."

Me and my big, fat, stupid mouth.

"But what about us? I thought… Don't we have something? You just said… You said you loved me. Was that a lie?"

His stunning emerald gaze locked on me. "No. I've never felt about anyone the way I feel about you."

"Then stay with me. I need you. I can't do any of this on my own."

"You can, and you will. You're the bravest, smartest creature in this, or any other world. You are powerful. You are limitless."

"But I'm not! I'm not any of those things. I'm scared of my own shadow, I'm clumsy. I talk waaaay too much and most people hate me."

"Nobody hates you."

"What about your brother?"

"Yeah, okay. Dusty hates you, and maybe Rebecca, and the vampires, and Donatella—"

"You're not helping," I said.

"Sorry." He hung his head.

My head was spinning, and the panic was becoming nearly

impossible to control. There had to be a way to get around this agreement he'd made.

"Okay, so then take me with you," I all but begged. "I'll be good, I promise. I won't even talk back...much, and I can help, you know, with all your royal stuff."

"You can't come with me any more than I can stay here. You have your own destiny to fulfill; your own important work to do. You're part of the Patrons now, they need you. They will look to you for guidance, to help those who dwell in the Inner World navigate a bold, new future. Not to mention that you're Vincent's new right-hand man."

I glared at him.

"Sorry. Woman. You're his new right-hand woman."

Talk about biting off more than I can chew.

"But I don't care about Vincent or the Patrons or the Inner World."

"Yes, you do, Clarissa. And they need you here as much as my people need me."

"That's debatable," I muttered.

"Plus, non-faeries, especially humans, are banned from our realm. Even if I tried, the Council would never permit you to enter."

"So, that's it? You're not even willing to try?"

Sonny shook his head slowly, and I felt the werewolf ire, vile and hot, rise from the pit of my stomach, ready to erupt. I had to use every ounce of self-control I had not to lash out and slap his face.

"Fine," I said, pushing away from him. "Go, then. Get the hell out of here and do what you have to do. I don't need you. I don't want you." I shoved him and he staggered two steps backward. "Get away from me. I hate you. Coward! Liar."

I saw the sadness in his eyes; could practically hear his heart breaking, but I was too mad to care.

"Dusty!" I shouted before I lost my nerve. "Moondust! Get

your ass back here right now! His *Royal Highness* is ready to go home."

Plumes of green smoke filled the room once again, and Dusty materialized.

"It's about time," he whined. "I've been stuck on the ethereal plain with your sister," he said, jutting his chin toward me. "She's even less pleasant than you."

"Seems we all have crappy siblings, then, doesn't it?" I said, scowling at Sonny.

"Whatever. Are we all done here?" Dusty asked, rubbing his palms together. "Time is of the essence."

Dusty glanced between Sonny and I and his gaze hardened. "Sunshine, it's time. Fix it," Dusty said, pointing at me.

Sonny glared at Dusty, and it was obvious then that there were still more surprises in store for me.

Oh, goodie.

"Fix it?" I asked but got no answer. "Fix *WHAT?*"

Sonny steadied himself. "You, um… You have intimate knowledge of me and the Faerie realm and, well, that's not permitted."

"So, what? Is fix it like a code or something? Is it a euphemism for killing me? Because, if that's the plan, it's pretty dumb considering you've spent the entire time I've known you fighting to keep me alive!"

Okay, so I was starting to panic a little. I mean, it's not like I was easy to kill, but it could be done. And if anyone knew how to do it, it was Sonny.

"Clarissa."

"I will fight back, you know. I'll fight back and kick your ass. I'm strong—"

"Clarissa, calm down. I have no intention of killing you. I would rather die than hurt you."

"But you are hurting me!"

"I can make you forget. I can make you forget everything."

"Like amnesia? Are you nuts?" I balked. "You're going to just wipe my memory and leave me defenseless against all the crazies just clamoring to kill me? I'd be a sitting duck. What is wrong with you...you...monsters?"

"Not amnesia," Dusty interjected. "It's more like mind control, like rubbing chalk off a blackboard to make space for new information. It's a neat little trick we Fae mastered. It's one of the ways we've managed to keep our existence a secret. And our race so pure."

"So, what will I forget, then?"

"Me," Sonny said. "Us. All your knowledge about the faerie realm. Even Dusty."

"Well that's no great loss," I said, and Dusty smirked. I think I was growing on him.

"Once it's done, you'll forget you ever knew me."

Now, my heart really was breaking.

"But I don't want to forget you. My memories are all I'll have once you're gone."

"There's no other way to protect you from the Fae armies who would use you to get to me, and the throne. They'll kill you, your family, anyone you've ever cared about—"

"Why does nobody know how dangerous you faeries are?" I all but screeched. "Everyone thinks you're all Tinkerbell and glitter. Instead, you're crazed, blood-thirsty ghouls."

"Good PR?" Dusty shrugged.

I chuckled through my tears and had to hand it to Dusty—his comedic timing was impeccable.

"Believe me, if I could think of another way, *any* other way, I'd try it," Sonny said. "But Dusty is right. You know too much, and that puts you in danger. I blame myself."

"I blame you, too."

I was overcome by a wave of exhaustion and utter despair, as I realized I was struggling to fight for something Sonny was just willing to throw away like yesterday's newspaper.

"So, what now?" I asked, conceding, too broken to think straight.

"Now, I wipe the board clean."

"Can you really do that?" I whispered, hoping that somewhere, deep inside himself, he'd find the strength to change all this.

"He can and he will," Dusty said. "And if he doesn't..."

"You will not so much as lay a finger on her," Sonny barked. "Or it'll be the last thing you do."

"Fine. Then just fix it yourself. Now."

Sonny faced me and brushed an errant hair from my face. I couldn't even begin to imagine how horrendous I must have looked, but he didn't seem to care. His eyes, so full of pain and sorrow, were fixed on mine, and I knew at that moment, he thought I was the most beautiful creature in the world.

Everything hurt; my head, my heart, my teeth from clenching my jaw so hard, every muscle in my body screamed from the tension coiled within them...and there was nothing I could do to ease the pain.

"Who's the last one?" I asked, trying to buy as much time as I could with him.

"The last one?" Sonny asked with a frown.

"Your last sibling. Dusty said there were six siblings. You, Dusty, Bram, Woody and June... Who's the last?"

Sonny inhaled deeply and shook his head. "This isn't the time to get up to speed with my family tree, Clarissa. This is serious."

"I want to know."

"You're just going to forget."

"No, I won't. I *will* remember. I'll remember everything. I don't care what you or Dusty or anyone else says. What we have is too important. I will never forget you or our time together."

Sonny lowered his eyes. "I wish that was true, but it's impossible—"

"Nothing is impossible. You'll see. You'll work your faerie king mojo on me, but it won't stick. It won't stick and that'll prove to Dusty and the rest of your family that I'm worthy of you. That I'm not just some failed experiment, some mongrel."

"It's me who has never been worthy of you, Clarissa."

I smiled and prayed to God that for once, my werewolf heart would work in my favor and make me immune to Sonny's faerie magic.

"Fine," Sonny said finally. "It's Stan."

I pulled back and looked into his eyes. "Your brother's name is Stan?"

"Yep."

"What's it short for? No, wait, let me guess. Is it ConSTAN-tinople?"

Sonny shook his head. "Nope."

"Fine. What's it short for?"

"Stanley."

"*Staaanley*? That can't be right."

"Why? Would you be disappointed if it was?"

"No, but I'd be surprised," I said.

"There's no fooling you, is there?"

I shook my head defiantly.

"Fine, it's short for Mustang Free."

I tried not to laugh but failed miserably. "Stan is definitely better," I said.

When my laughter finally subsided, Sonny gently touched his forehead to mine, took me by the hands and laced our fingers together.

Adrenaline surged through me. It was time.

"Will it hurt?" I asked.

He ran the backs of his fingers down my damp cheeks before cradling my face. "You won't feel a thing."

"I find that hard to believe," I sniffled.

"Trust me," he said.

"Yeah, right."

Sonny looked deep into my eyes, and a feeling of dread coursed through me. This was it. I could see it in his face. In a moment he was going to cast a spell and wipe any memory of himself from my mind, but one thing I knew for certain, he could never wipe the indelible impression he'd made on my heart.

"Close your eyes," he whispered.

"No! I'm not ready!"

"Yes, you are. Close your eyes."

Choking back the tears, I did as he instructed.

"Goodbye, Clarissa," he whispered. "I love you." His lips feathered gently over mine. It was all I could do not to sag to the floor.

"I won't forget you," I whimpered. "I promise."

"You promise?" I felt him smile against my lips.

"Yes," I whispered. "Cross my werewolf heart."

EPILOGUE

"OH, NO YOU DON'T," Miss Rebecca snapped as I cut across the grand foyer and made a beeline for Vincent's office. "You can't go in there."

I stopped in front of the reception desk and peered at the wiry woman perched behind it. I noted the way she recoiled ever so slightly under my scrutiny, but much to my surprise, Rebecca wasn't even the teensiest bit afraid of me. In fact, judging by the pungent smell of sour milk and burning rubber wafting from her direction, I'd say she was angry and [sniff sniff] possibly a little repulsed.

But definitely not afraid.

"Tell me," I said, setting down my backpack and propping my elbows on the counter in front of her. "Why exactly is it that you hate me?"

Rebecca's lips thinned and one fuzzy brow arched.

"Come on," I said, slapping the sweetest smile I could muster on my face. "You know you're just dying to get it off your chest."

She took a steadying breath, and for a minute, I actually thought she was going to do it; spill her guts, and maybe, finally, tell me why she disliked me so much.

I braced myself for the onslaught, a little giddy with anticipation, if I was being honest.

"I don't hate you," she said, somewhat unconvincingly.

Nuts. No onslaught.

"I just don't understand why everyone thinks you're so special."

I cocked my head. "Who thinks I'm special?"

"Like you don't know."

"Pretend I don't."

"Fine," she sighed. "The lycans, the sanguisuge."

"Hardly a fan club worth bragging about, now is it?" I replied.

"Vincent. Azrael. I hear the gnomes like you. And…there are others," she said with more spite than the situation warranted.

"But not you?" I said, pointing at her.

"No, I don't think you're special at all. In fact, I find you quite…ordinary."

I thought about myself, my numerous flaws and foibles, my propensity for yammering, my weakness for Ben and Jerry's, my inability to wrangle my own cat or keep a tidy house, and decided she was right.

"I accept that," I said, bending down and picking up my backpack. "I'm definitely nothing special."

"And yet they treat you like you're the second coming."

"Maybe I am?" I pondered out loud.

Rebecca snorted.

"No, seriously. I mean, I've come back from the dead like a gajillion times. I have superpowers. I can communicate with spirits, well, one spirit, but whatever. I just might be the next messiah."

"If you're the messiah, I'm the Queen of the Damned," Rebecca muttered.

"Ohmygod, are you? Because that would actually explain a lot. The BO and facial hair alone—"

"You can't even begin to imagine what I am," Rebecca rumbled in a way that made my skin crawl. "So, don't push your luck, Ms. Hunt."

And then she growled. Literally.

Could.

Not.

Get.

Away.

From.

Her.

Fast.

Enough.

However, no sooner had I taken a step toward Vincent's office, she snarled at me again, louder than the first time. "I told you, you can't go in there. I have strict orders—"

I raised my hand. "I think we both know I'm not much for orders—strict or otherwise."

"Vincent's directive was very specific. He was not to be disturbed, under any circumstances, by anyone or anything."

"Well, seeing he thinks I'm *soooooooo* special." I smirked (yes, I was being cowish, but she deserved it). "Let's just presume his directive doesn't apply to me."

"I'm pretty sure it does."

"Let's see, shall we?" I waggled my fingers at her as I backed toward the office door.

I hadn't expected Rebecca to flip me the bird, but I was kind of glad she did because:

1) I deserved it, and

2) I finally felt like we were making progress.

•

The moment I stepped into Vincent's office, I understood why Rebecca was so adamant I shouldn't enter. Vincent had a visitor—an enormous, imposing, and might I say, *haaawt*, visitor with sparkling emerald eyes and a gaze so intense, it made me squirm a little.

"I'm sorry," I said, clearing my throat. "I didn't realize you had company."

Vincent scowled. "Rebecca should have advised you—"

"Oh, she tried," I said, shuffling farther into the office. "But you know me." I smiled and offered a little shrug.

The tall stranger had yet to take his eyes off me, which was kind of cool, but also kind of gave me the wiggins. There's staring and then there's *star-ing*.

"I'm sorry, but have we met?" I asked, stepping forward and extending my hand to the new guy. "My name is Clarissa."

"I'm sure we haven't," he said, barely acknowledging me or my outstretched hand.

Vincent subtly positioned himself between me and the green-eyed, albeit boorish, hunk-o-burning love. "His Highness is here to discuss matters pertaining to the Faerie Kingdom," Vincent said.

"Private matters," Ol' emerald eyes added.

"You're a faerie?" I gaped, suddenly feeling quite ridiculous standing there with my hand sticking out, especially when the Faerie King clearly had no interest in shaking it.

#introfail

Vincent motioned to my extended arm and shook his head in a way that suggested I was doing something wrong. So, I promptly dropped my hand back to my side and straightened.

"Not big with the handshaking, I see," I said. "You're not the only one. Funny story, when I first met Vincent—"

"No," the massive faerie said before turning his back on me

and whispering something to Vincent in a tone so hushed, not even my super-sensitive werewolf hearing could pick it up.

I needn't have bothered straining myself, though. Turns out they were speaking some weird faerie language I didn't understand.

"Rude much?" I mumbled, causing Vincent to flash me his trademark *Oh, for the love of God, woman, please just shut up* look. So, I stood back, crossed my arms and mentally cataloged all the ways I could kill the arrogant son of a Faerie Queen and dispose of his body by feeding him to Aunty Brigit's pigs. Maybe I could ship him off to Aunty Gwen's? She didn't have any pigs, though. She had the alpacas. They're not carnivorous, are they?

After what seemed like an eternity, Vincent and Baron Von Boofhead (it seemed like an appropriate nickname for His King-liness now that I'd gotten to know him better), disengaged from their tête-à-tête, and not surprisingly, the grumpy faerie cast me a withering glare.

"Would you like me to leave?" I asked.

"Very much," the Faerie King said, stony-faced.

"Then you're in for a big disappointment," I replied, making my way over to my favorite overstuffed chair and plopping myself down on it.

"That's fine," he sighed. "We were just leaving."

I glanced around. "We?"

He raised one perfect brow and pursed his lips.

"Oh. Was that a royal we?" I asked. "Sorry, I'm just not accustomed to speaking with people who talk about themselves in plural."

I searched his face for some kind of reaction, even the smallest twitch or smirk. But I got donuts. Nothing. Niente. My gut was telling me there was more to this man, but he was so smooth, and cool, and blisteringly handsome that he was throwing my spidey-senses all out of whack.

"I'll be damned if I'll ever understand what he sees in her," His Royal Highness muttered, glancing at Vincent, and shaking his head.

He made sure to use English that time, the bastard.

"We'll be in touch," the grumpy faerie said, shaking Vincent's hand and as expected, completely ignoring me.

What in the hell had I done to annoy him so much?

Before I could even open my mouth, His Kingliness snapped his fingers, instantly filling the office with thick plumes of emerald smoke and *poof*! disappearing before my eyes.

Seconds later, all that remained was the potent smell of apple pie, and more glitter than you'd expect to see at Mardi Gras.

At least he smelled better than Rebecca, but then again, my FOGO bin smelled better than Rebecca.

"So that's the Faerie King, hey? Isn't he the charmer?"

"He's not the king," Vincent said, swatting at the lingering smoke and coughing. "The king is in Keijujen Valtakunta, the Realm of the Fae. That was the king's brother, Commander of the Faerie Armies and their representative here within the Order."

"And he's an uppity schmuck."

"The Fae are quite renowned for being…uppity," Vincent said, glancing over his shoulder, like he was looking at something, or someone, behind him.

I craned my head to get a better look, but there was nothing there.

"You okay?" I asked, but Vincent didn't respond. So, I leaned forward and waved my hand in front of his face. "Hello?"

"I'm sorry, what?"

"Are you okay? You seem…weird."

He raised his brows. "Weird?"

"Weirder than your usual weird. Distracted."

"It's nothing."

"Oh, I get it. Secret faerie business. What did Prince

Charming want, anyway? Tips on how to win friends and influence people? Do tell."

"What part of *secret* did you not understand?"

"Fine. Can you at least tell me what he meant?"

"Meant by what?"

"Before, when he said he didn't understand what *he* sees in me. What *who* sees in me?"

"Can't say I know," Vincent said, busying himself with some papers, but not before he glanced over his shoulder again.

"You know I can tell when you're lying, right?" I said.

"I'm sure you can," Vincent replied.

"Okay. Whatever. You keep your little secrets. I don't even care."

"I'm sure you don't."

"Could you be any more condescending?"

Vincent glanced up at me. "Yes. No. What? I mean, pardon?"

I shook my head. It was obvious something was going on, but he clearly wasn't in a sharing mood. But it was okay. I could wait. I'd gotten very good at waiting.

"What's his name, anyway?" I asked.

"Who?"

"Who do you think? Baron Von Boofhead, who else?"

"Baron Von—where do you even come up with these nicknames?"

"I'm creative." I grinned. "And what is his name? Unless you want me to address him as The Baron from now on?"

"It's Moondust."

My brows disappeared into my hairline. "I'm sorry, what?"

"His name is Prince Moondust Glow."

I snorted. "Seriously? That giant, hunka-hunka burning love is called Moondust?"

"And you find that amusing?"

"Well, yeah. Don't you?"

"Not particularly. What do you think he should be called? Conan, perhaps? Thor?"

"Well, at least they're names more befitting royalty."

"Befitting?"

"You know, regal, distinguished…masculine. Moondust is hardly the name of a king, is it?"

"He's a prince."

"Whatever. I'm just saying, his name lacks a certain credibility."

"Perhaps to you. But remember, Clarissa, not every species measures a man's worth by how masculine his name is or isn't perceived to be."

"Yeah, yeah, it doesn't say much for the human race. I've heard it before." I paused then and looked at Vincent.

Wait. I *had* actually heard that before.

Verbatim.

But where?

And from whom?

I couldn't remember talking to Vincent about faeries before, apart from that one time when he gleefully informed me that everything I thought I knew about the glittery imps was grossly inaccurate. They were more likely to gut you than grant you a wish. I couldn't thank him enough for those nightmares, let me tell you.

"Are you alright?" Now it was Vincent's turn to flap his hand in front of my face, clearly concerned by my extended and uncharacteristically long silence. "Clarissa?"

"I have the strangest feeling of déjà vu," I said, blinking at him.

"Like a premonition?"

"No. Like I've had this conversation before."

"Oh. I see. Perhaps it's a new werewolf power?"

I snorted. "As far as wolfy powers go, it's pretty underwhelming," I replied, shaking my head. "I mean, déjà vu, big whoop."

"Still, better than a tail," Vincent said with a smile.

"You can say that again." I nodded.

"Still better than a tail."

I smiled. I liked it when he loosened up.

"So, will his Royal Highness be rejoining us anytime soon?" I asked, as casually as I could. "I can hardly wait for him to show up and ignore me all over again."

"You needn't worry. The fae don't like being here amongst the humans any more than we enjoy having them. It'll be some time, if ever, before you see him again."

"Excellent, because that guy is enough to make me barf." Total lie, of course, but I wasn't about to tell Vincent that. "Now," I said, pulling my laptop from my backpack and walking to Vincent's desk. "Scooch over."

"Scooch?"

"Yes. Move your butt. Shift it. We have work to do."

Vincent stayed where he was, as if riveted to the spot.

"Make a little space for me, please? You've got all the room in the world over there." I pointed to the vast expanse of desk space immediately to his right.

"But I like it here. It's the best place for…um… For…"

I rolled my eyes. "Just stop being a desk-hog," I said, giving him a little shove, surprised when he almost toppled over. No, not toppled, more like ricocheted off something—something that wasn't there—and just about fell on his butt.

"Are you sure you're okay?"

He shook his head. "I'm fine."

He was so not fine. If he was fine, I was Salma Hayek.

I glanced at my watch; 6:22 p.m. Shoot. I was going to be late. "Alrighty then, let's get to work."

"You're in a hurry," Vincent said. "What's the matter, got a hot date?"

"As a matter of fact, I do."

No sooner had the words left my mouth, a large, gilded picture frame sailed off the wall behind Vincent, whizzed past his head, and crashed to the floor at our feet, sending tiny shards of shattered glass skittering across the hardwood floors.

I raised my brows. "What the hell was that?"

"What was what?" Vincent said, pretending he hadn't noticed the flying decor that nearly took his head off.

"Um, the airborne photo of you and…" I picked up the picture, brushed off the broken glass and peered at it. "Who even is this?" I turned it to face him.

"Michael J Fox."

I shrugged. "Never heard of him,"

Vincent's eyes widened. "How can you not know who Michael J Fox is?"

"The same way you don't know who Lizzo is."

"Now there's a household name."

"It is for anyone born *this century*," I replied.

"He's quite a famous actor, you know."

"Who?"

"Michael J Fox."

Seemingly someone was put out by the fact that I had never heard of this Michael J guy.

"*Back to the Future. Family Ties.*"

"Yes, yes. I'm sure he was quite the celebrity back in the day."

"Back in the day? What in heaven's name are you talking about?"

"It's okay. No need to bore me with all the details. I'd much rather you explained the deal with the flying Fox photo." I motioned to the shattered glass smattered all around us and was overwhelmed by déjà vu again.

That was going to get old very quickly.

"What's going on?" I said, patience waning. "Something's off today. Faerie Dust poofing in and out like a giant douche, picture frames flying through the air, and you're all weird and twitchy. I smell a rat."

Actually, I smelled ripe peaches and jelly lollies, but I wasn't about to tell Vincent that. It was a familiar smell, a comforting smell. It was also kind of a sexy smell that immediately had me feeling all squirmy and warm. I liked it. Hence, I said nothing. Not often, but from time to time, I knew when to keep my mouth shut.

"I told you, Prince Moondust was here on official faerie business. I'm fine, maybe I'm coming down with a cold or something."

"Can you even catch a cold?"

"I'm human. I assure you I can catch a cold."

"Wait, it's not COVID is it?" I said, covering my nose and mouth with the sleeve of my cardigan. "Take a RAT."

"It's not COVID. It's just a cold. And as for the frame..." He glanced around. "Well, you see, there's been a lot of seismic activity in this area of late."

"As in, earthquakes?"

"Um, yes?"

I wondered if he'd intended it to sound like a question.

"I don't recall any—"

"We're nine levels down, Clarissa. We're far more susceptible to seismic tremors than top dwellers."

Top dwellers. Well, that was new.

"So, earthquakes caused the frame to fly off the wall?"

"Yes. No. Sort of."

"Well, that clears things up."

"If you'd let me finish," he sniped.

"Be my guest," I said. "I'm dying to hear this."

"Well, the last tremor dislodged one of the air-conditioning ducts and with all the aftershocks...and...and...increased magnetic activity and the updrafts—"

I raised my brows. "Updrafts?"

"Oh, yes. Many updrafts. They're causing all types of problems."

"Like making random items fly around the office?"

"Yes. Exactly. Just yesterday, my Gandalf just about took Rebecca's eye out."

"Your *what*?"

He gestured at his precious LoTR chess set. "Gandalf."

I kept forgetting, for a super-cool immortal badass, he was a ginormous nerd on the inside. He probably came from Middle Earth in the first place.

"And then there was the um… The, er—"

I held up my hand. "You know what? If you don't want to tell me the truth, that's fine," I said. "But you don't have to make up these cockamamie stories. You should have just told me it was a ghost or something. At least I might have believed that."

Vincent visibly sagged. "Yes, well, that would have been a much simpler explanation, wouldn't it?" he said, pinching the bridge of his nose.

I shook my head. "One day you might trust me enough to be straight with me. I mean, I managed to trust you, even after all the crap you've pulled."

Vincent actually looked hurt, and uncomfortable, and guilty. Good.

"Anyway, you were saying?" Vincent continued. "Did I hear correctly? You have a date tonight?"

"Don't sound so surprised. Some people do actually find me interesting and attractive."

"Yes, I'm sure they do, but isn't it a bit soon?"

"A bit soon after what?" I asked. "Seriously, I don't think I've so much as smiled at a man since all this crap started, and I'm over it. Old ladies in nursing homes get more touch than me."

"That's a little bit of an exaggeration, don't you think?"

"No. I've literally had zero action in six months. It's like I'm invisible to men."

I was contemplating exactly when it was that I last had sex, or fooled around even, when I noticed a supremely gross smell wafting around the office. It was kind of like Rebecca's bin juice perfume, only ranker.

I lifted my left foot, and then my right, inspecting the soles of my shoes.

"Problem?" Vincent asked.

"Do you smell dog poop?"

He sniffed. "Can't say I do."

"What about bin juice? Can you smell bin juice? I feel like it's coming from—" I peered over his shoulder.

"Clarissa, I don't smell anything." He straightened and widened his stance.

"Well, I can and it's coming from there." I pointed to the empty space behind him. "Wait, maybe it's from all the seismic activity? Maybe all the earthquakes loosened your sewage pipes?"

"Or, perhaps Rebecca has a new smelly candle thing?"

"A candle that smells like dog shit and liquefied garbage?" I paused, and Vincent at least had the decency to look ashamed of his lying ass.

"You know what? Poop-scented candles sound about right today. I mean, it's either that, or I have a brain tumor."

"I doubt—"

"Wait, they can't kill me anymore, can they?" I asked.

"Brain tumors? No. They cannot."

"Excellent, then I'm not going to worry about it."

I spread myself out on Vincent's desk, extracting my laptop, an iPad, a mouse, and a Bluetooth keyboard from my backpack. I also pulled out a brand-new notebook, some extra-large sticky notes and a packet of markers in rainbow colors.

The puzzled look that crossed Vincent's face was priceless.

"Tools of the trade," I said, preempting the *what the hell is all this crap?* question I knew was coming.

"I'll take your word for it," he said.

Vincent was uncharacteristically quiet as I set up the equipment and logged on to the internet.

"With whom?" Vincent asked, trying to seem casual, but failing miserably.

"I beg your pardon?"

"With whom are you going on a date?"

"No one."

"I don't believe you can call it a date if it's just you, a bucket of *Chooky Chicken* and Netfish, Clarissa."

"Firstly, it's Net-FLIX, you social leper. Secondly, Chooky Chicken? Pah-lease. I refuse to eat a product that's loaded in saturated fat—"

"I saw you eating some last week."

"*Anymore*," I said, remembering the double bacon chicken burger I'd devoured after a particularly stressful episode that involved getting Miss Miranda off the third-floor balcony before she made a leap for freedom. "And thirdly, if you won't tell me what Moonface was doing here, then I don't see why I should divulge any details about my love life to you."

"Love life? You're in love?" he said, jerking forward like he'd been shoved off the high dive board at the Sunshine pools.

"Oh, God no. It's just an expression. I thought it was more appropriate than saying sex life."

Another photo frame sailed off the wall and smashed against the back of the office door. I waited for Vincent to react, but he completely ignored it like it never happened.

And so did I.

"Why are you even dating now?" Vincent said. "You know the timing isn't ideal."

I cocked my head. "And why's that?"

"You have so much else to focus your energies on right now:

your work here with the Patrons, coming to terms with your new werewolf traits, and let's not forget solving the mystery of how you ended up with Dante's heart. I just think you have enough on your plate without adding romantic entanglements to the mix."

"Well, when you put it that way, what sensible, red-blooded woman wouldn't want to spend all her time nine stories underground searching for black market organ traders on the internet? Or worrying about the next deranged beastie that might want a shot at lopping my head off? Why on earth would I possibly want to go out for a meal, and maybe a little dancing, with a charming, intelligent, sophisticated man? Partake in some scintillating conversation, a bit of flirting—if I even remember how—and maybe, just maybe, get myself a little well-deserved sexy time?"

"Please never say sexy time in my presence again," Vincent said, screwing up his nose. "I just meant it's advisable—"

"Thanks, but no thanks," I said. "Remember, I don't have to listen to your lectures or answer to you. You're not my dad. You're not my grandpa. You're not even my grandpa's grandpa's grandpa."

"I was just making conversation," Vincent sulked.

"Pfft! Just making conversation, my ass. You were one hundred percent stickybeaking, and don't even bother trying to convince me otherwise. You're not fooling anyone, Vinnie."

"How many times do I have to tell you not to call me Vinnie?"

"At least one more," I said with a wink.

I flipped open the laptop and opened the new website and blog I'd been developing for the Patrons. I wanted to show Vincent all the work I'd been doing since he employed me.

"You know who needs a date?" I said, sliding him a little side-eye.

"No. Just no," he replied.

"You."

Vincent huffed. "I don't date."

"I know, but you should."

Vincent glared at me. "You wouldn't be saying that if you knew my situation."

"I'm well aware of what happened to you. You lost the love of your life and were cursed to walk the earth for all eternity. I know you think this would make a romantic relationship tricky—"

"Impossible."

I snorted. "If I've learned anything from this whole experience, it's that nothing is impossible. Don't get me wrong, I'm not saying relationships haven't been difficult for you in the past, or that they won't be tough going forward. But it's been like a million years. When are you going to move on with your life and put all that behind you?"

Vincent's eyes filled with a melancholy that was hard to look at, and I immediately wanted to punch myself in the face for being such an insensitive cow.

"Probably never," he said.

"That's what I figured. It's a shame, though. You're such a good catch. You'd make some lucky lady very happy."

I was surprised when Vincent's cheeks turned a rosy shade of pink, and he shook his head.

"What? It's true. You're smart, you're a very snappy dresser, and you're not exactly hard to look at."

Vincent rolled his eyes.

"And what woman could resist your debonair style, sparkling wit, or dazzling personality?"

I was relieved when his eyes softened, and a warm smile split his handsome face.

"You know I have a couple of friends—clients actually— well-groomed, independently wealthy, a little high maintenance, though. You know, fillers and Botox, the not negotiable expectation that you'd get them into the Birdcage during Spring

Racing Carnival, that kind of thing. But nothing you couldn't handle."

"The Birdcage?"

"Anyway, I could arrange for a meet and greet—"

Vincent shifted from one foot to the other and I could see by the paled expression on his face that I'd one hundred percent overstepped.

"You know what?" he said. "I'm the boss. I don't have to answer to you or anyone else about my love life."

I snorted. "Okay. Just keep that in mind the next time you're overcome by the urge to give me a lecture about mine."

Vincent shook his head.

"Anyway, since neither of us is in the mood for a girlie chitchat, why don't we get a wriggle on? We have lots to do and I have areas I need to wax."

This time, a first edition of the complete works of Shakespeare sailed off the bookshelf and landed on the desk about twenty centimeters in front of us.

I looked at the book, which had dropped open on the first page of *Romeo and Juliet*, then looked at Vincent. His expression was cool and impassive.

"We just going to pretend that didn't happen?" I asked.

"Ignore it," he said, without even looking at me.

I pursed my lips, then nodded. "And the smell? The smell that reminds me of anger and regret and jealousy. Should I ignore that, too?"

"If you don't mind."

I took a deep breath and nodded. "Is this anything I need to worry about?" I asked. "Are you in danger?"

Vincent shook his head.

"Am I in danger?"

He shook his head again.

"Fine, but you owe me an explanation. One day."

"Indeed," he agreed. "One day."

ABOUT THE AUTHOR

Esther Del Zuanne is a mentor and communications specialist who love, love, loves to write lively, paranormal romantic comedies. Her heroines are bold and brash with boundless energy and tonnes of pizazz - and a dash of sass thrown in for good measure. Her heroes are daring, brave, super-sexy and oh, so, cheeky… Impossible to resist and easy to love.

Esther's debut *Cross My Werewolf Heart* trilogy, is the first in her **#fangsfurandfreaks** series, based on the misadventures of Clarissa Hunt and the mysterious Patrons of Order - keepers of the thin veneer that separates humanity from the seething supernatural world on its doorstep.

When she's not writing about things that go bump and growl in the night, Esther spends her time going to rock concerts, cruising **realestate.com** for beach-front properties she'll never afford, and watching her favourite horror movies over and over and over again.

She's been married to the Rock God since 1996 and lives in Melbourne, Australia, with two fur babies, waaaaay too many cushions (or so she's been told) and an embarrassing collection of Buffy the Vampire Slayer memorabilia.

Esther also loves hearing from readers and other writers. You can find all her contact details, social media links and sign up for her newsletter, by visiting **estherdelzuanne.com**

9 780645 897838